The Shado...

Other Books by Debbie Viguié

The Shadow of Death

Psalm 23 Mysteries

By Debbie Viguié

Published by Big Pink Bow

The Shadow of Death

Copyright © 2014 by Debbie Viguié

ISBN-13: 978-0990697107

Published by Big Pink Bow

www.bigpinkbow.com

All rights reserved.

This is a work of fiction. Names, characters, places, and incidents
either are the product of the author's imagination or are used
fictitiously. Any resemblance to actual persons, living or dead, is
purely coincidental.

To Calliope Collacott for her tireless support

Thank you to everyone who helped make this book a reality, particularly Barbara Reynolds, Rick Reynolds and Marissa Smeyne.

1

Detective Mark Walter's attitude about holidays was completely dependent on whether or not he was working them. Holidays had a remarkable way of bringing out the best in people and the worst in people. He loved the celebratory feeling of time off that he could spend with his wife, Traci. He hated being called to a crime scene when a family function had gone horribly, horribly wrong.

The Fourth of July was coming up in just a couple of days and already he was bracing himself. He wasn't scheduled to be on call that day, but he had a terrible niggling feeling in the back of his brain. It didn't help that since meeting Cindy and Jeremiah holidays had seemed to become a focal point for murder, or, at least, the discovery of it. He knew it wasn't the secretary and the rabbi's fault, but they did have the most astounding knack for stumbling over dead bodies. What made him even more nervous was that they hadn't found one for months. They were overdue.

So he had taken matters into his own hands. He had invited them both to a barbeque at his house to celebrate the holiday. That way he would know where they both were, and maybe could relax and enjoy the day instead of waiting for the inevitable call from one of them. Traci told him he was being paranoid. He thought he was being proactive. All of that didn't stop the terrible feeling that something was going to go wrong, though.

"Mark?"

"Yeah, sorry," he said, turning to his partner, Liam. It was still hard not to think of Liam as his new partner even though they had been working together now for ten months. He was a good man and he'd had Mark's back, the only one who had been willing to take on that role after the death of Mark's previous partner, Paul.

Mark hadn't made any more progress for months on solving the mystery behind his late partner's life. The truth was, he was struggling very hard to put the past in the past and focus on the future. Namely he was focused on the upcoming birth of his and Traci's first child. It was going to be a girl. That was one mystery he could not wait to have solved. Traci, on the other hand, still didn't know. She wanted to be surprised, but it was getting harder every day not to spill the beans by accident.

Mark took a deep breath. "What were you asking?"

"What should I bring to the barbeque tomorrow? I could make a potato salad or something."

"No, Traci makes that. It's her mom's recipe and it's the best I've ever had."

"A fruit salad then?"

"That could work."

"How many people are going to be there?"

"Eleven. Twelve if Traci's younger sister comes, but I doubt it."

"Okay."

Contrary to popular belief, not all Mark's days started off with a fresh dead body. Actually very few of them did. While some cases were pretty open and shut, many were more complicated than that. In truth, the majority of his time was spent working the angles and trying to solve cases that had been open for more than a couple of days. In that way he envied the detectives on television. Always a new crime to solve and always a nice, neat ending forty minutes later.

Mark picked up the next file on his desk with a sigh. It was an unsolved murder almost two years old at this point. He flipped it open and found himself staring again at a picture of a guy with dark, curly hair, olive skin, and intense eyes. He was an Iranian named Asim Kazmi who had just turned twenty-one when he was murdered. He had been a student at one of the local colleges and had been murdered in the park downtown. A female jogger had found him dead, sitting up on a park bench with a knife buried in his chest.

There had been no fingerprints as it turned out. None anywhere. Not even on Asim's fingers. His fingerprints had all been burned away post-mortem. It made no sense really. Whoever had killed him had taken the time to remove his fingerprints, but not his wallet, which included a school issued picture i.d. among other things. Teachers at his school and his passport, which they found in his apartment, also corroborated his identity.

The fingerprint thing had always bothered him. It was incredibly suspicious and there were only a handful of reasons that he could think of why someone would bother to do that. As the investigation had continued and they hadn't found anything concrete, Paul had kept urging him to let the fingerprint thing go, saying it was a dead end.

He couldn't help but wonder if Asim's fingerprints had been intact what would have happened if he had run them. Would they have shown up but under a different name? If Asim was an alias and his killer was trying to obscure his real identity it would make sense. It also made sense why

Paul, himself an imposter, kept telling Mark to forget about the fingerprints.

There it was again, the doubts about Paul, the second guessing of everything he'd said or done in light of the revelations about him after he'd died. He tried to keep himself from doing so because that path lead to madness.

"You look a bit on edge," Liam said.

Mark grimaced. It was getting to the point where Liam could read him frighteningly well. "A bit," he admitted.

"Why don't you go home? It's late, and I've got things covered."

"After I read through this file I'll head home."

He flipped through the notes he'd made. Interviews with students and faculty at the school had been less than helpful. Everyone he had interviewed had described Asim as either "nice" or "shy" or both.

He read again the notes of his interview of the female jogger who had found the body. No new insights there. He flipped over to start reading Paul's notes. Paul had made detailed notes about the crime scene and had talked to a few other bystanders, none of which had been any help. Seeing Paul's handwriting didn't improve his mood. What made it worse was the man wrote like he spoke so Mark could almost hear his voice reading the words out loud.

He was just about to close the file and take Liam up on his offer when something caught his eye. Paul had made a notation that he believed a homeless man with a German Shepherd had seen something, but refused to talk about it.

The hair on the back of Mark's neck lifted as he wondered if that would be the same homeless man who had been found dead months later in Jeremiah's front yard. If so, was that his German Shepherd that Jeremiah had

4

adopted? Thanks to Joseph's charity program there were several homeless people in the area who had dogs, but they had acquired them well after Asim was killed. The only homeless man he was aware of that had had an animal prior to that was Peter Wallace, the man who had turned up dead on Jeremiah's lawn.

Even though that homeless man had been killed at the same time that several others had, the killers had never confessed to his particular murder. Was it possible he was killed not by them but by whoever had killed Asim? If so, the fact that he was killed so close to Jeremiah's home and died in his yard became much stranger.

Mark stood up abruptly. "I need to get some air."

"I told you, go home," Liam said without looking up from the file he was studying.

Mark should have listened the first time. He grabbed his coat and headed out to the parking lot. After climbing into his car he put the key in the ignition but didn't start it. He just sat for a moment, staring out the windshield at nothing while his brain went into overdrive.

Could the homeless man really have been killed over what happened to the student? If so, why was there a several months gap between the two? And what did Jeremiah have to do with any of this? Mark was starting to think that it was too much of a coincidence that the homeless man had died on the rabbi's lawn.

Peter Wallace had been the homeless man's name. Mark and Paul had gone to the funeral, as had Jeremiah. Mark had noted that a couple others attended as well, but that they stayed far back from the activity and didn't interact with anyone. Peter, Asim, Jeremiah. What, if any, was the connection between the three of them?

5

Mark felt suddenly very tired. Being on the brink of solving a puzzle, especially one he'd been working on so long, usually energized him. Not this time, though, and he had to admit to himself that it was because of Jeremiah. He knew the man had a past but up until now Mark had done his best to avoid knowing too much about it. He had figured it was better for everyone that way. There was a phrase for that...plausible deniability. What he didn't know couldn't hurt any of them.

His phone vibrated and Mark pulled it from his pocket. Traci had texted him asking him to pick up more potatoes and sparklers at the store for her on his way home.

Potatoes and sparklers. That's what life was all about. One was commonplace, everyday life. The other was special, unexpected, a highlight that broke through the mundane and transformed things if even just for a moment. The average person would get to see about 80 Fourth of July celebrations if they were lucky. That was less than 3 months of celebration and sparklers in a lifetime.

"Life is too short," he said out loud as he gently pounded the steering wheel with his fist. At this point he was one of the only, if not the only, person who cared about finding Asim's killer. Or Peter's for that matter. There were no families or friends pressing him for answers, begging for justice. He wanted that justice for them, but he was beginning to worry that it might come at a terrible cost. He closed his eyes and breathed in deeply, trying to calm his thoughts. In the words of one of Traci's favorite songs, he should let it go.

He opened his eyes, started up the car, and pulled out of the parking lot. He wasn't sure he could let it go forever, but for the moment he was off duty and there was a party to prep for, a holiday to celebrate, sparklers to bring joy. He'd deal with life's potatoes later.

As it was he managed to go to the store, buy sparklers, and get back to his car before realizing he had forgotten to buy Traci the potatoes she needed. *Apparently I can let something go*, he thought ruefully as he went back in for the potatoes.

At work Cindy Preston watched the minutes on the clock drag by. She was sitting at her desk in the church office waiting for her day to be done so she could get out of there. She kept hoping one of the pastors would come in and tell them to take off early. In hopeful anticipation of that she was ready to go. All she would have to do was shut down her computer and grab her purse.

"You're so antsy you're making me antsy," Geanie said. "What on earth is up with you today?"

"I just wanted to get the long weekend started. It's the first I've had in a while."

"Memorial Day was only a few weeks ago."

"Yeah, but I got stuck working at the all church picnic the new pastor decided to have."

Their permanent new head pastor to replace the one who had quit had been there for three months now. Ben was nice, outgoing, and the best part was he and the music director got along. Maybe a little too well. They had been busy planning all kinds of new events, which was great for the church, but an incredible amount of work for Cindy and the rest of the staff.

"I know we're seeing you tomorrow at Mark and Traci's party, but what are you doing the rest of the weekend?"

"I'm not sure about later in the weekend but tonight Jeremiah and I are going to watch Independence Day. He's never seen it before."

"Aha! Movie date is what has you so excited."

"It's not a date," Cindy protested, feeling herself flush.

"Right," Geanie said, drawing out the word sarcastically.

It wasn't. Although, Cindy didn't know what it was. For the last few months they had been in this weird place. It was odd, sometimes knowing Jeremiah's secret made them seem closer and sometimes she could still feel him holding her at arm's length.

They still didn't talk about his past, not really. She wanted to, but he was always hesitant. She figured maybe it was too painful. Although she had to admit that on her own time she had taken a sudden intense interest in spy movies. Jeremiah might not want to talk about his past, but her curiosity was growing by the day. That coupled with the fact that things had been very quiet lately were helping to set her on edge. She felt like she was in this constant state of anticipation.

Waiting for the other shoe to drop. That's what her dad would say. She just wondered how long she'd have to wait.

"What are you and Joseph doing?" Cindy asked, trying to change the subject.

"First Fourth of July as husband and wife," Geanie said with a grin. "We're totally going to celebrate that."

Cindy laughed. "It's my understanding that you and Joseph are pretty much celebrating every minute of every day this year."

"And why not?" Geanie asked with a flip of her hair. "It isn't everyday a guy lands a fantastic catch like me."

The door opened and they both stopped laughing. The Youth Pastor, Dave, also known as Wildman, came charging in with a look of complete rapture on his face. He walked up to them and then came to a stop. "Amazing news everyone!" he said, eyes shining. "You'll never guess."

"Then don't make us try, tell us!" Geanie said.

"I was in a meeting all afternoon with Ben talking about the youth program here at the church. Where it is, where I want to see it go, everything."

"And?" Cindy prompted when he stopped talking.

"He said yes!"

She blinked in confusion and turned to glance at Geanie who also looked puzzled.

"To what exactly?" Cindy asked.

"To the thing I've wanted to do since I started working here!" Wildman crowed triumphantly as if it should be instantly obvious what that was.

He was usually not this difficult to get a straight answer out of, but clearly he was very excited and agitated about whatever it was. As a Youth Pastor he had to be up and act excited all the time. Of course, the thing that really got him charged up was...

"Oh," Cindy said, suddenly having an inkling of what he was talking about.

"Yes!" he said, grabbing her hands and shaking them up and down. "Can you believe it?"

"I'm still not following," Geanie confessed.

Cindy turned to look at Geanie. "What is the one holiday that the two of you share an intense passion for?"

Geanie's eyes widened and she leaped to her feet with a shriek of joy. "Really?" she asked, running out from behind her desk to shake Dave's shoulders hard.

"Yes, really!"

The two of them began bouncing up and down in uncontrollable joy.

The business manager's door flew open and a moment later Sylvia poked her head out, a scowl on her face. "What on earth is going on here? I was on an important call and I had to tell him I'd call him back."

"Amazing news, Sylvia," Geanie half-shouted before Dave even got a chance to speak.

Sylvia looked from Dave to Geanie and back again. Then she groaned and slumped against the wall. "If both of you are this excited then that can only mean one thing."

"That's right," Dave confirmed. "We're going to have a Halloween party!"

2

Jeremiah was on edge. The worst part was that there was seemingly no reasonable cause for it. The truth was he had been on edge for months, ever since Martin's friendly warning back in Las Vegas that retired Mossad agents were being reactivated. He knew he was probably being paranoid. After all, the odds that his former employer would want to reactivate him were a long shot. No, they had retired him for a reason and it was hard to even fathom a reason why they would reverse that.

Cindy had asked him why he had retired. He hadn't given her a real answer to that question which he knew frustrated her. There was no way to talk about that without talking about what he did, though, and he really wasn't ready for that conversation.

Sometimes he wondered if he was making things too complicated. Cindy had feelings for him. Of that he was certain. If he asked her to he was sure he could get her to stop asking questions about the past he'd left behind. That wasn't fair to her, though. Still, he was either going to have to do that or start coming up with things he didn't mind revealing about that past.

Captain padded into the kitchen and nuzzled his hand. Jeremiah scratched him behind the ears and the dog gave a sigh of pleasure. Animals were easy. People were difficult.

He was making deviled eggs to take to the barbeque at Mark's. They would keep overnight and this way he wouldn't have to deal with them in the morning. He had just finished arranging them all on a platter and was getting ready to put it in the refrigerator.

"Want a taste?" he asked the dog, lowering the spoon he'd been using so Captain could lick it clean.

His mother who made deviled eggs for practically every get together would not have approved. She would have told him that he was spoiling the dog. That was okay. Captain deserved a little spoiling. He was a good dog and life before he had come to live with Jeremiah could not have been easy.

"Mark said you could come with me tomorrow and play with Buster. Would you like that?"

Captain wagged his tail, whether at the prospect of seeing Buster or the hope of having some more deviled egg Jeremiah didn't know. He put the spoon in the sink and scratched Captain's head again. "And you can have a deviled egg tomorrow at the party."

He glanced at the clock. Cindy should just be getting off work soon. Time to clean up and head over to her house for movie night.

When he pulled into his driveway Mark still hadn't been able to shake the dark thoughts that kept clouding his mind. He turned off the engine and sat for a moment, drawing deep breaths. Since finding out that Traci was pregnant, he had been working hard not to take his work home with him either physically or emotionally. She needed less stress in her life. Truth was, it had been a welcome reprieve for him as well. Slowly but surely he'd been working on truly leaving work at work and not stressing about his caseload while he was home. Traci deserved a husband who wasn't a basket case half the time.

He flipped down the mirror that was on the back of his visor and stared at his own reflection. "There is nothing weird about Jeremiah," he told himself solemnly. "You're just looking at a lot of circumstantial evidence and that doesn't necessarily mean everything lines up. He's just a normal guy."

No matter how convincing he sounded, he still didn't believe it. There was a connection between the rabbi and the homeless man who had died in his yard. It was possible Jeremiah didn't realize it and truly hadn't known the man, but Mark was convinced that where the man had ended up was no accident.

The front door opened and Traci stuck her head out. She must have heard the car and been wondering what was taking him so long. He smiled and waved at her. She crooked her finger at him, summoning him inside. Careful to keep the smile on his face he got out of the car. He retrieved the things from the store and headed inside.

"How's the most beautiful pregnant woman ever?" Mark asked before giving her a kiss.

"Better now that you're home," she said, leading the way to the kitchen.

The baby wasn't due for another two and a half months but Mark could swear that she was ready to burst. The kitchen, which had been pristine that morning, looked like a bomb had gone off in it.

"You've been busy," Mark noted as he set the groceries down.

"I'm trying to get as much as I can done now so that I can relax and have fun tomorrow."

"Good idea. How can I help?"

"You already have," she said, as she pulled out the potatoes he had purchased. "So, what's got you upset?"

Mark shook his head. For some reason ever since she had been pregnant Traci had been so much more in tune with his emotions. That was one of the reasons he had tried so hard in the car to settle himself down.

"Just working through all the angles of a cold case," he said.

"Is it Paul's?"

"No."

"Then why are you upset?"

Mark took a deep breath. "I found a possible link that I don't like."

She turned from the sink where she had begun peeling the potatoes. "Does it connect to Cindy or Jeremiah?"

"You guessing that because they keep popping up in so many cases the last couple of years?"

"No, I'm guessing that because there aren't that many people you like well enough to care if they were connected to a case."

Despite his mood that got him to chuckle. It was true. The list of people he would call friends was short. "You've got me there."

"Look, I know that a lot of bad guys tend to get killed when Jeremiah is around, whether or not he's actually responsible for that."

"You've noticed?"

"How could I not? Particularly after your diatribe during the cattle drive."

"You know what they say," Mark muttered. "Where there's smoke there's fire."

14

"You know what they also say?" Traci countered.

He shook his head.

"People who play with matches get burned." She turned back to the sink and continued peeling potatoes.

"So, you don't think I should take too close a look?"

"You don't think you should or you would have by now. That's good enough for me."

"Sometimes being friends with a person can be a real pain in the butt."

"Being married to some people can be even more so," she said.

He could hear the smirk in her voice. "Okay, fine. No more thinking or talking about work until Monday."

"Better. Now help me peel these potatoes. I need to sit for a few minutes."

Traci was right. She always was. Now if he could just let it go before he saw Jeremiah at the barbeque everything would be fine.

Both Geanie and Wildman were still beside themselves with excitement. Cindy instinctively knew that their excitement coupled with the prospect of a three day weekend ensured that no more work was getting done that day at First Shepherd.

"What exactly did Benjamin agree to?" Sylvia asked, folding her arms across her chest.

"He agreed to let us put on our own Haunted House maze!" Wildman said, still bouncing up and down in time with Geanie who was laughing and clapping her hands together like a three-year-old.

Sylvia's eyebrows shot up in surprise. "Really?"

"Really! As long as all our scenes depict Biblical events."

"Isn't that going to be a little limiting for a Haunted House?" Cindy asked.

Sylvia nodded. "Don't those things usually have characters more in line with vampires, psychotic clowns, and serial killers?"

"Normally, yes, but I've got it all worked out. Just imagine, a recreation of Jael hammering the tent nail through Sisera's head and blood spurting everywhere!"

Sylvia shook her head and glanced at Cindy. "I don't think Benjamin knows what he's let us in for."

Cindy nodded as Dave went on to describe more horrific scenes that he had planned. Sylvia let him talk for a few more seconds and then she raised her voice.

"On this...exciting...note, I think it's time that we close up for the day."

Cindy couldn't have agreed more. Thirty seconds later her computer was turned off, her purse was on her shoulder, and she was out the door. She would have enough time once she got home to change clothes before Jeremiah arrived.

Three blocks from the church she stopped at a red light. A bicyclist pulled up next to her. He leaned over and tapped on her passenger side window startling her. He spun his hand in a circle indicating that she should roll down the window. Cautiously she hit the button and lowered the window a couple of inches.

"I just thought you should know that it looks like your back tire on this side could use some air. It looks pretty low," he said.

"Oh, thank you," she said.

"You're welcome. Light."

She glanced back at the streetlight and saw that it had turned green. As she pulled her foot off the brake she turned to say thank you again, but the bicyclist was already on his way through the intersection.

Cindy stepped on the gas and pushed the button to raise the window. She'd have to look at the tire once she got home. Hopefully it wasn't too bad since the low air pressure warning light hadn't come on. She had a pump in her trunk. Then again maybe she could convince Jeremiah to do it for her. She felt a smile tugging at the corners of her mouth. It was handy to have a guy around sometimes.

A few minutes later she pulled into her driveway and parked. She walked around to the back of her car and inspected the rear tire on the passenger side. It did look low, though not as much as she had anticipated. It wouldn't take but a minute or two so she decided she might as well get it over with.

She retrieved the air compressor from her trunk and then opened the passenger front door so she could plug it into the charger. She paused as she noticed that there was an envelope in the footwell. Cindy frowned as she picked it up, trying to figure out when she could have dropped it there. She turned it over and froze. What looked like Hebrew words were scrawled on the front in a handwriting that she didn't recognize. It read *malakh ha-mavet*. She tried saying them out loud, but there was nothing familiar about them.

Could Jeremiah have dropped the envelope in her car the last time he was in it? That was certainly the most logical conclusion, but that had been more than a week ago. Surely she would have noticed it before now if he had.

Maybe it had been under the seat and just now slid out to where she could see it. When he got there she'd ask him about it.

She put the envelope down and plugged in the compressor. After adding air to the one tire she double checked the other three which all seemed to be okay. Finished, she put the compressor back in the trunk, grabbed her purse and the envelope, and headed into the house.

She dropped her things on the kitchen counter, washed her hands in the sink, and then hurried to her bedroom to change clothes. Since they were going to be watching Independence Day as a pre-Fourth celebration she opted for jeans and a red and white striped shirt. She had a T-shirt with the flag on it, but she'd be wearing that the next day to the barbeque at Mark and Traci's. As soon as she was dressed she went into the bathroom where she ran a brush through her hair and reapplied some lipstick.

She made it to the family room just as the doorbell rang. When she opened it she was surprised to see Jeremiah holding a bouquet of red, white, and blue flowers.

"For me?" she asked before she even bothered to greet him.

He smiled but he looked uncomfortable. "I saw them at the store earlier and thought they were too festive to pass up."

"They certainly are," she said, taking them from him and then stepping back to let him enter. She hurriedly got a vase out from one of the cabinets and filled it with water. She got out her kitchen scissors and cut the stems on the diagonal before rearranging the flowers in the vase.

She carried the arrangement to the coffee table and put it down in the middle. "It looks beautiful," she said.

He smiled at her, but didn't say anything.

"Shall we order a pizza?" Jeremiah asked.

"Sounds like an excellent an idea," she said. She went to the kitchen and grabbed her phone from her purse. After placing the order she hung up and put the phone down on the counter next to the envelope she had discovered earlier.

"I was wanting to ask you about something I found in my car this afternoon," she said, picking the envelope up and carrying it back into the family room.

"In your car?" he asked.

"Yeah. I've never seen it before and I have no idea how it got into the car. What do you make of it?"

She handed it to him, curious as to what the writing on it meant. "Can you read what it says?"

Jeremiah stared intently at the writing on the envelope. A muscle in his jaw twitched for just a moment. "Where did you say you found this?" he asked, his voice definitely strained.

"On the floor of the front passenger seat of my car when I got home tonight."

"And you're positive that's the first time you saw it?"

"Yes, of course. Why?"

"Were all your doors locked when you got out to the church parking lot this afternoon?"

"I think so. They should have been. When I came back from lunch I locked all the doors. I assume they were that way when I came back to the car. I know the driver's side was for sure," she said. He was making her increasingly nervous and she didn't like it. "Jeremiah, what is it?"

"Did anything strange happen today, anything even remotely out of the ordinary?"

"Yes, the new pastor gave Wildman permission for the youth group to put on a haunted house event for Halloween. Shocked us all."

He shook his head. "No, not like that. Were there any people you didn't know hanging around the church interacting with you in any way?"

Cindy thought back over her day, trying to ignore the fact that the longer Jeremiah went without telling her what he was thinking the harder her heart was beginning to pound.

"The UPS guy who delivered to the office today wasn't the regular guy. He chatted for a minute, asked me a couple things about the church. Apparently he and his wife are looking for a new one."

"Did he give you anything or say anything out of the ordinary?"

"He just gave me a package for our business administrator. It was some books she had ordered. There was nothing special about it and I signed for it like I always do. And no, nothing he said seemed strange. It just sounded like he was genuinely interested in knowing a bit more about the church."

"And he didn't ask you anything personal?"

"No, nothing. Jeremiah, what's going on?"

"That was the only interaction you had with a stranger today?"

"Yeah, I ate at the Mexican restaurant down the street that has the giant burritos, and I've had that waitress tons of times."

"There's nothing else you can think of?"

"Oh," she said, as another thought hit her. "A bicyclist pulled up beside me when I was driving and told me that my back tire needed air."

Jeremiah leaned forward, eyes boring through her. "What did he look like?"

"I don't know. He was wearing a bike helmet so I couldn't see the color of his hair. He was tan, athletic."

"Did he have any kind of accent?" Jeremiah asked.

Cindy shook her head. "Not that I could tell."

"Did he say anything to you besides telling you about your tire?"

"No, and I didn't even really have a chance to say thank you. The light turned green and he was off before I knew what happened."

"Did you roll down the window to talk to him?"

"Only a few inches," she said. "He was on the passenger side of the car.

"Did you take your eyes off of him for even a second?"

"He told me the light had changed and I glanced forward, saw it was true, and when I turned back he was already on his way."

Jeremiah was looking increasingly pale.

"Please, tell me what it says," she entreated, pointing to the envelope he was still clutching in his hands.

He looked down at it, then back up at her. "It's Hebrew. The translation that would capture the meaning of it is 'Angel of Death'."

3

Jeremiah stared at the envelope, feeling sick to his stomach. Why had someone thrown it into Cindy's car? He was convinced it had to be the bicyclist. That moment she looked away from him to see the traffic signal he could have easily dropped it in.

"Was your tire actually flat?" he asked.

"No, just low on air."

"But not low enough that you noticed when you got in your car?"

"I don't normally look at my tires before getting in the car. It wasn't enough to set off the low tire pressure sensor, though."

"How about your other tires?"

"They were fine. Why?"

He hesitated, trying to decide how much of his suspicions to share with her. The bicyclist could have easily let air out of that one tire while she was at work, giving him the excuse to ride up beside her while she was on the road. Doing it to a tire on the passenger side of the car guaranteed that if she was an average driver she wouldn't notice it before leaving the parking lot. He could have just told her that her tire was low without going to the trouble, but then when she went to fill it up she would realize he had been lying and would instantly have been suspicious of him and his actions. As it was he had done his job so well she hadn't even thought about him being the one to place the envelope in her car.

Had the cyclist broken into the car at the church and put the envelope inside then, there was a good chance she would have noticed when getting in the car and realized that something was wrong, at which point she could have easily called the police. Having the envelope suddenly appear when she got home did the trick of making her think that it had somehow been in her car for a while, perhaps under the seat. So she hadn't called the police but had instead given him the envelope thinking that since it had Hebrew writing on it that it was probably his.

It was very clever, but it was also a completely round about way to get to him. He felt his chest tighten as he wondered if this was going to signal a new rash of attacks on Cindy by someone linked to the man who had been trying to hurt her months before. When he had killed that man at Geanie and Joseph's wedding he had warned that others would be coming.

He had a dilemma. He didn't want to scare her, but he couldn't leave her completely in the dark and unprotected. She was staring at him intently and he was going to have to tell her something.

"I think it would be a good idea if you stayed with friends for a couple of nights, just to be on the safe side."

She glanced at the envelope in his hands and she grew noticeably paler. "The people that you said might try to hurt me again, you think this is a message from them?"

"I don't know what to think at this moment, but I don't want to take any chances with your safety," he said.

"I'm sure I could stay with Geanie and Joseph."

Jeremiah shook his head. "Joseph needs to upgrade his security system. Too many people have managed to sneak onto his property in the last couple of years. I wouldn't feel okay about that unless you had around the clock police protection, too."

He had been one of those who had managed to sneak onto Joseph's property and he'd been grateful at the time that the security system had holes in it. He really should talk to Joseph about upgrading, though. Him being able to sneak into the house was one thing, but it was just too vulnerable right now.

"Okay, if not them then who do you suggest I stay with?"

"Mark and Traci." It was the best solution. If he was going to trust her to stay with anyone else it would have to be with someone who had a gun and knew how to use it if it came down to that.

"Okay," she said slowly. "And just what do I tell them about why I need to stay there? I mean, do we tell Mark about the envelope?"

"No," Jeremiah said emphatically. This was definitely not a matter for the police. "I'll figure out something to tell them. In the meantime, let's get you packed."

When the pizza arrived half an hour later Cindy had just finished getting a suitcase ready. She hated to impose on Mark and Traci, especially with Traci being pregnant. Jeremiah wasn't one to jump to worst case scenarios, though, and if he said she shouldn't be by herself then she believed him.

She just wished he would tell her why.

24

While she had packed he had paced like a caged tiger. He'd finally settled down after borrowing a magnifying glass and had been at the kitchen table perusing the envelope ever since. She wasn't sure what he was looking for, but he didn't seem to be in the mood to overshare.

It was frustrating, but she also knew that if she pushed for answers at this point he'd close up even more. Patience was her best option.

They ate dinner in relative silence. It drove Cindy crazy, but she managed to keep herself from pushing even then. As soon as he was done eating he pulled his phone out of his pocket and called someone.

"Hello, Mark. It's Jeremiah."

Cindy couldn't hear Mark's side of the conversation even though she strained. She'd just have to settle for hearing what Jeremiah was going to say.

"No, noone's dead," Jeremiah said, sounding even more serious than usual. "Yes, looking forward to the party tomorrow. Look, I need a favor. Cindy's place has gotten some pests. There's an exterminator that's going to handle things, but she needs somewhere to stay for a couple of nights."

There was a pause in which she still couldn't hear the other side of the conversation.

Jeremiah scowled. "That's not funny. You know that's not approp-"

Cindy couldn't help but wonder what on earth Mark had proposed.

"Yes, tonight...No just her...Okay, see you then."

Jeremiah hung up and turned to her. "It's fine with them. They just asked that we wait for a couple of hours

25

before heading over so they've got time to prep the guest room."

"Well, unless you're ready to talk about what's going on, then I suggest we watch the movie."

For a moment she thought he was going to object, but then he nodded and headed over to the couch to sit down. She put the movie in and settled down to watch.

Unfortunately, even though she enjoyed the movie, she realized she was only half-watching. Her brain was far too busy trying to figure out what was up with the envelope. She knew she was going to be obsessing about it until they had some sort of concrete answers about its meaning, and who had thrown it in her car, and why they had done so. She just hoped they could get it all resolved quickly so she could get on with enjoying her weekend instead of stressing out over it.

She could tell Jeremiah was distracted, too. She would have just given up on the movie and told him they'd watch later, but they had to do something to kill time while waiting to go over to Mark and Traci's.

She did manage to finally focus toward the end of the movie just in time for the president's speech which always brought tears to her eyes. Jeremiah seemed to appreciate it as well.

At last the movie was over and Jeremiah carried her suitcase out to his car while she turned off lights and locked up. As she did so she thought about the fact that one of these days she was going to need to get a security alarm. She probably should have gotten one years before, but the need had become overwhelmingly obvious.

They spent the drive in silence, each one of them occupied with their own thoughts. It was just a few minutes, but it seemed much, much longer. At last they arrived. "Well, I guess we're just going to have to start the party early," Cindy said, attempting to lighten the mood.

"You can never have too many fireworks," Jeremiah said.

"Words to live by."

Mark answered the door. "So, this little pest problem...is it something we should be canceling the party over?" he asked with a smirk.

"Oh no, not at all," Cindy said fervently.

Jeremiah remained silent. Mark didn't like the look on his face, though. Something was very, very wrong and it had nothing to do with household pests. He stepped back to let them inside.

Traci waved enthusiastically from the couch where she had retreated to put her feet up. "Sorry, I overdid it a bit," she apologized.

"Oh no, you should rest when you need it. And while you can," Cindy said with a warm smile.

Mark took Cindy's suitcase from Jeremiah. "I'll put this in the guest room," he said.

Cindy nodded and sat down next to Traci. Buster enthusiastically gave her a welcome lick. The two women were quickly engrossed in baby talk as the baby began to kick and Cindy got to feel it.

Mark took the suitcase back and put it down next to the bed in the guest room and then hurried back into the family room. Jeremiah was standing just inside the door, unmoving, his eyes fixed on Cindy.

Mark grabbed Buster's leash from its peg next to the door. "Come on, Buster. The men are going to take a walk," he said with a significant look at Jeremiah.

Fortunately the rabbi didn't protest, just followed them out of the house. The three of them hit the sidewalk. It was slow going as Buster felt the need to thoroughly sniff every mailbox.

"So, what's really going on?" Mark asked without preamble. "If Cindy needs police protection for something there are easier, more efficient, more correct ways to go about it."

"They're also more official," Jeremiah said. "This doesn't need to become official."

"I have to admit, I'm not liking the sound of this," Mark admitted. Try as he might he couldn't keep his suspicions about Jeremiah and his connection to the homeless man from rearing their head.

"I'm not asking you to like it, but I am asking for your help."

Mark stopped while Buster inspected yet another mailbox. "Is what's going on connected to those things you and I don't talk about?" he asked bluntly.

Jeremiah gave him a small, humorless smile. "It might be. That's what I need to figure out."

"And you felt Cindy would be safer here with a cop than at Joseph and Geanie's?"

"Something like that."

"You know, one of these days you and I are going to have to talk about those things we don't talk about."

Jeremiah looked him dead in the eyes. "I pray that day never comes."

"Unless one of us is killed I think it's inevitable at this point."

Something dark flashed in Jeremiah's eyes and then vanished. Mark blinked, wondering what exactly it was he had just seen. The rabbi usually wore a pretty impenetrable mask, but Mark had the uneasy feeling that he'd just had a glimpse beneath it. He was sure that he never wanted to see that look again from anyone, let alone from Jeremiah.

He shook his head. "I've got a bad feeling that a reckoning day is coming, Samaritan."

The corners of Jeremiah's mouth quirked up. "You haven't called me that in a while."

"At least, not that you've heard," Mark said, struggling to backpedal from the edge of a precipice. He realized his hands were clenched into fists at his side. So were Jeremiah's. They were standing, facing each other, almost sizing each other up as though they were enemies ready to fight.

But he knew enough to know that he would never want Jeremiah for an enemy. He just hoped the day never came when he couldn't have him as a friend.

"How long do you expect Cindy to be with us?"

"Hopefully just a day or two. It might be longer, though."

"If it's longer than that I have a feeling we'll all be needing police protection."

"Some of us, at any rate," Jeremiah said.

Mark shook his head. "See, when you say things like that it doesn't make me feel better."

"It wasn't designed to."

"You know, I think it was easier back in the good old days when you pretended like you'd never been anything but a rabbi."

"Then you should have stopped asking questions a long time ago."

"You know that's not in my nature." Mark sighed. "But, no more questions for now. Cindy can stay with us for as long as she needs to."

"Thank you."

"Let's get back to the ladies."

They turned and walked back to the house.

"Is there anything you need that I can get you?" Mark asked.

"No. I've got it covered," Jeremiah said.

Back inside the house they discovered that Traci was giving Cindy the tour of the nursery that they had just finished painting. They had opted to go with a pale, soothing green on the walls since Traci didn't know the sex of the baby, and they both agreed that they liked green better than pink or blue anyway.

"Looks like you've just about got everything done," Cindy commented.

"The crib and dresser were gifts from Mark's parents," Traci said.

"When is the baby shower?" Cindy asked.

"Next month. My older sister who you'll meet tomorrow is putting it on."

A strange look crossed Jeremiah's face.

"What is it?" Mark asked him.

Jeremiah shook his head. "It's just strange to me. For Jewish people, we don't have baby showers or set up the nursery before the baby comes."

"Why not?" Traci asked.

He hesitated a moment and then said, "In our culture, it's seen as bad luck."

"You set up the nursery after the baby comes? During all that chaos?" Mark asked.

"Yes. I mean, often after the baby is born while mother and child are still in the hospital the husband would come home and set everything up so it would be ready when they arrived."

Mark shook his head. "I'm going to be a basket case when the baby happens. This furniture took me an entire day to assemble. I can't imagine how I would have deciphered the terrible directions that came with them under that kind of pressure."

"I see the logic of that. It's just odd to me," Jeremiah said.

Mark laughed ruefully. "In this case I prefer my brand of odd to yours."

Jeremiah stayed a few more minutes before excusing himself. He would be back the next day by noon for the festivities. In the meantime, he had some things he wanted to work out.

He made it home and walked inside, carrying the envelope that he had taken from Cindy's house. He was hoping he could learn more about it.

Jeremiah studied the envelope intently. Other than the words there were no other markings. It was a standard white envelope, the kind you bought in bulk at any grocery store or drug store.

He put a pot of water on the stove and waited until it was boiling. Once it was he carefully held the envelope in the steam, waiting a minute to see if any other writing appeared. When none did he carefully pulled apart the seams of the envelope, spreading it out until it was just a flat sheet of paper. He was hoping to find something, a microdot, a word, anything.

There was nothing. It made no sense. Why bother to write the words on the outside of an envelope if there was nothing else meant to go inside? Why not just write them on a small slip of paper?

He turned off the stove, took the paper, and sat down at the kitchen table. Captain padded up to him and put his head on Jeremiah's knee. He scratched behind the dog's ears.

"What do you think, boy?"

The dog just squeezed his eyes shut.

Jeremiah put the envelope down on the table, close to Captain's head.

A moment later the dog jerked. He opened his eyes and a deep, menacing growl rose up from his throat. He lunged and grabbed the envelope with an unearthly howl of rage.

4

Captain shook his head violently, as though the envelope was some creature he had caught and was trying to kill.

"Captain, stop!" Jeremiah shouted, stunned at the dog's outburst. He reached over to try and take the envelope away from him, but Captain jumped away. He stood in the middle of the kitchen, chewing and shaking until all that was left of the envelope was little bits of paper scattered on the ground. Finished, Captain walked back over and laid down at Jeremiah's feet, whimpering.

Jeremiah reached down to pat him on the head and Captain flinched. "Easy boy, it's okay."

There was only one thing that Jeremiah could think of that could have made Captain freak out like that. He had had a similar reaction a few months before when he encountered the man who had killed his previous master. That man was dead, though. Jeremiah had seen to that.

Still, before he died the terrorist had told Jeremiah that there were more of them out there, waiting. Was it possible that there had been two people present when Captain's former master had been killed? Was the scent left on the envelope intentional?

If so, it was a very convoluted way of sending a message. Cindy had to find it and show it to him. He then had to take it home to look for extra clues and put it somewhere his dog could get a good whiff of it. There were too many steps for it to be an effective plan. There were too many places where it could go awry. That just made the whole thing even more confusing.

One thing he hadn't been able to figure out yet was why Peter, Captain's former master, had been killed. He doubted that the man's real name had been Peter despite what the identification on his body had said. When Jeremiah had met him he'd been going by a very different name, and he had been a spy working for the C.I.A. How Peter had gone from being a top operator in Iran to a homeless man in California he didn't know.

The question was, why had he been killed? And why had he been killed on Jeremiah's street? The man had made it as far as Jeremiah's yard before collapsing. What would he have had to say if he could only have made it to the door? Was he killed because he knew Jeremiah and someone was afraid of what he might tell him? Or was Peter killed for some other reason, something he'd known about from his past or even something he'd uncovered in his present? How was he connected to the men who wanted Jeremiah dead? It was possible they were Iranian and their revenge on Jeremiah was related to something that had happened in that country. If that was the case it was possible that they had had it in for Peter as well.

There were too many pieces of the puzzle still missing. What was worse was he didn't know how to go about actively searching for those missing pieces without raising red flags all over the place.

Retirement was not shaping up to be as low-key and uneventful as he had been hoping for. In fact, his whole carefully constructed house of cards was threatening to fall down around him.

He finally decided to give up for the night. Maybe his subconscious would come up with the answer if he got some sleep and allowed it the chance to work on the problem. He threw the now useless paper bits into the garbage. He got ready for bed with Captain pressed next to him the entire time, nearly tripping him twice.

When he finally got in bed the dog crawled up to lay next to him, pressed against him, instead of at his feet where he usually slept. Jeremiah put his arm around the animal and gently stroked his back. He whispered softly to the traumatized animal and eventually the tension left Captain and he fell asleep. Just as Jeremiah drifted off he realized that he had been speaking to the dog in Hebrew.

Cindy woke the next morning early with a sense of excitement and trepidation. It was Independence Day and it should be a great party as long as they didn't have any uninvited guests. She got dressed in her jeans and her flag shirt and made her way to the kitchen. Even though it was early she found Traci already up.

"You're up early," Traci commented.

"Not as early as you apparently."

Traci grimaced. "The baby was kicking a lot this morning, all over the place."

"I guess it wanted to start celebrating the holiday with a bang," Cindy said, smiling.

"She."

"She? It's a girl?"

Traci nodded.

"Congratulations! But I thought you were waiting to find out when it was born," Cindy said.

"That's what I wanted. Mark insisted on knowing."

"And he couldn't keep it a secret?"

Traci sighed. "No, he's trying. He's been very careful to say gender neutral terms only."

"Then how do you know?"

"Because even though he's a fantastic detective he would make a lousy criminal. He telegraphs everything. I can't go into a baby section of a store with him without him gravitating straight to the girls' clothes."

"I'm sorry," Cindy said as she sat down at the kitchen table and leaned over to squeeze Traci's hand.

"It's okay. I can still pretend to be surprised, which is what I'm going to do."

"Well, I had no idea until now that you actually knew," Cindy said.

"That's because I'd make a far better criminal than my husband."

"Or actress," Cindy said with a smile.

"That too."

"So, what can I help with today?" Cindy asked, changing the subject.

"I've got almost everything under control. Of course, when it gets closer to time I'll need help setting up the tables in the backyard and carrying out the food."

"Then I'll take that on as my job. You really should be taking it easier than you are."

Traci rolled her eyes. "You're beginning to sound like Mark. Honestly, I'm pregnant, not helpless."

"I'll try to keep that in mind."

"What's the deal with you and Jeremiah? Has he kissed you yet?"

The question caught Cindy off guard and she felt herself blushing. "No!"

"Then you should kiss him," Traci said. "One of you has got to go first."

"I would never kiss him first," Cindy protested.

"You know, it always amazes me how many things people think they'd 'never' do. When the chips are down, that list is usually a lot shorter than people like to admit."

"I wouldn't. I believe the guy should make the first move. Besides, there are no moves to be made here."

"You are such a liar."

Cindy felt herself flushing more. "There are things that are in the way."

"Like what?"

"Like religious differences for example."

"Okay, what else?"

"Well, I don't know..."

"Aha! Nothing else, just religion," Traci said triumphantly.

"Isn't that enough?"

"Not in my book," Traci said as she got up and got herself a glass of orange juice. "Want some?" she asked, indicating the carton.

"Please."

Traci brought two glasses of juice back to the table and sat down. "You know what my rule for dating was? Three strikes and they're out."

"What in your book would constitute a strike?" Cindy asked after taking a sip of her juice.

"Anything that for you would be a large negative. When I was dating I considered smoking a strike. Excessive drinking, considerable age difference, and being divorced were all strikes as well. There were others, too. If a guy had three of those strikes they weren't worth pursuing. It sounds like Jeremiah only has one in your book."

"Yeah, but it's a big one."

"Christians and Jews worship the same God, don't they?" Traci asked.

"Yes, but-"

"Then what's the problem? It's not like he worships someone or something else."

"The problem is that Christians accept God's forgiveness through the sacrifice of Jesus who we see as the Messiah. Jews don't."

Traci frowned and took a swallow of her juice. "I thought some Jews did."

"Sure, there are some who do and they're called Messianic Jews. They accept Jesus as the Savior without abandoning their other religious traditions and beliefs. They're certainly the minority, though."

"And I take it Jeremiah isn't one of those?"

"No, he's not."

"And this is an issue because if you got married and had kids how would you raise them, and then when you die will you see each other in heaven or not, etc.?"

"That pretty much sums it up."

Traci took a deep breath. "Okay. I'll give you two strikes for that one since it would also potentially impact your kids. But that's it."

Cindy sighed and drank some more orange juice. Traci and Mark weren't religious. How could she expect them to really understand?

"Have you tried talking to him about Jesus? You know, get him to see things your way?"

"Not very much," Cindy admitted.

Traci rolled her eyes. "What's wrong with you? You Christians are supposed to run around converting anyone who will stand still."

"I haven't tried to convert you," Cindy said, exasperated.

"Maybe you should," Traci said, arching an eyebrow.

"I believe in leading by example," Cindy said, suddenly feeling defensive.

"Which is all well and good, but what happens when someone wants to actually talk to you about your beliefs?"

"I'm always willing to tell people about God and Christ."

"Really? Because here I am practically begging you to give me more information and you're being pretty close-lipped about it."

Cindy blinked in surprise. "You're asking me about my religion?"

"Yes, and you're not giving me a lot of information."

"You know, pregnancy has made you a lot weirder."

"And a lot more aggressive. Just ask Mark," Traci said with a smirk.

"Okay, what do you want to know?"

"Everything. You're the first close friend I've had who is a Christian. And, don't get me wrong, I love the fact that you're not all preachy, but I really want to know more about what you believe."

"You know, that was an incredibly tortured way to get to that question. You didn't have to tease me about Jeremiah first."

Traci grinned. "Oh, I totally had to tease you. Besides, Mark and I have a bet going about you two and I was looking for some inside scoop."

"Unbelievable."

"Not really. Tell you what, let's make some pancakes and you can tell me all about what you believe."

"Deal," Cindy said. The day hadn't even really started yet and already this was shaping up to be the most eventful Fourth of July she'd ever had.

The two women talked as they made breakfast with Traci asking a lot of good questions. Just as they were setting pancakes and bacon on the table Mark walked into the kitchen still sleepy looking.

"Something smells good," he said with a yawn.

"Breakfast," Traci said.

"What were you two talking about?"

"Oh, you know, the usual kind of girl talk. Life, death, the afterlife and how God fits into it all," Traci said with a serene smile.

"Wait, what?" Mark asked, squinting at her.

Cindy couldn't hold back a laugh at his expression.

"Never mind, dear," Traci said, kissing him on the cheek.

Breakfast turned out to be a hilarious event with Traci and Cindy teasing Mark mercilessly about anything and everything. Cindy couldn't remember the last time she had laughed so hard, and it felt so good. She'd never realized just what a wicked sense of humor Traci had.

After they'd cleaned up, Cindy started setting up card tables and chairs in the backyard. It was a nice size and it was fenced so Buster split his time between running around the yard and trying to figure out what she was doing. She tacked down the flag themed disposable plastic tablecloths. Thinking of the beautiful flower arrangement she had left at home on her coffee table she got permission from Traci to pick some flowers from the yard.

She soon had more than enough flowers and arranged them in vases as centerpieces on the tables. It was going to be a warm day. There wasn't a cloud in the sky.

She headed back into the house to finish gathering together the rest of the things she'd need for the tables but wouldn't be taking outside until it was almost time to eat. Mark was in the kitchen prepping the hamburger meat.

"What are you adding in?" she asked.

"Onion flakes, some garlic powder, and truffle salt."

"Oh, wow, that sounds amazing."

"They should be. It only took me seven years to get the recipe just right," he said.

"I'm sure it was well worth the wait."

The doorbell rang.

"That would be Traci's older sister and her family. They are always on time for everything. No matter what," Mark said with a sigh.

"I'll get it," Cindy said, heading off to the front door.

A woman with shoulder length chestnut colored hair looked shocked when Cindy opened the door.

"Hi, I'm Cindy and welcome to Mark and Traci's home!"

"Cindy? The sister of *the* Kyle Preston?"

"The one and only," she said, struggling not to grimace.

The other woman's face lit up. "I've heard so much about you and your brother. I'm Amber, Traci's older sister." She held out her hand.

"Nice to meet you," Cindy said as she shook hands with her.

"This is my husband, Doug."

"Nice to meet you," Doug said quietly as he shifted a serving dish to his left hand so he could shake with his right.

"And our twins Andy and Andrea. They're six."

The little boy and the little girl both said a shy hello.

"Well, come in everyone," Cindy said, standing back. She closed the door after them.

"Hello!" Traci said as she came down the hall.

Andy and Andrea ran to get hugs squealing "Aunt Traci!"

After hugging them both Traci said, "Why don't you two go say hi to Buster? He's in the backyard."

The kids hurried outside and Cindy smiled as she heard their shouts of joy and Buster barking excitedly.

Traci quickly hugged both Amber and Doug. "How are you both?"

"Doing good. I see that you're about ready to pop," Amber said referencing Traci's belly.

"It certainly feels like it."

"I'll go put the green bean casserole in the oven to keep warm," Doug said as he headed for the kitchen.

"You haven't heard anything from Lizzie, have you?" Traci asked her sister, her expression turning serious.

"I talked to her briefly a couple of days ago."

"Any chance she's coming today?"

Amber shook her head. "She's doing something with her coven."

Traci made a face. Cindy remembered that Traci had once told her that her younger sister Lizzie had started studying Wicca but then had shifted into something darker, more dangerous. Cindy had been keeping Lizzie in her prayers off and on since then. She was secretly relieved, though, that Traci's youngest sister wouldn't be making an appearance at the barbeque.

From the kitchen she heard a sudden burst of laughter and couldn't help but wonder what Doug had said to make Mark laugh. Outside the kids were still laughing. Amber was touching Traci's stomach and talking about babies. For just a moment Cindy felt suddenly very alone.

The emotion somewhat blindsided her. She struggled to shake it off. She didn't have a family of her own yet, but she would someday. Everything that Traci had said to her that morning about Jeremiah came roaring back into her mind.

A sudden knock on the front door startled her and she quickly moved to answer it. It was Liam, Mark's partner, and he was carrying a massive bowl of fruit salad.

"I think it will take an army to eat all this," Cindy said with a grin as she took the bowl from him.

"Well, I just doubled what I would normally make for myself," Liam said with a wink.

Cindy carried the bowl into the kitchen and set it on the counter. It looked like Mark was just about finished with the hamburger patties and he had pulled some hot dogs out of the refrigerator. She felt herself salivating when she realized they were Casper brand hot dogs.

She headed back into the family room just in time to see Liam walk out into the backyard, a tennis ball in his right hand.

Traci just shook her head. "He's going to get Buster and those kids riled up."

"They've all three got energy to burn. Maybe this way Andy and Andrea will actually sit still through lunch."

"Why, Amber, I never knew you believed in miracles," Traci teased.

"Car just pulled up. I think it's Jeremiah," Mark called from the kitchen.

Excited, Cindy headed for the door. She walked outside just as Jeremiah was parking across the street. She walked up to the car and gave him a hug when he got out.

"Everything okay?" he asked as he held her tight.

"It is now," she muttered against his chest.

"I'm not the last one here, am I?"

"No, you're right on time."

Reluctantly she pulled away, breaking the embrace. "Did you figure anything out...about the envelope?" she asked.

"No, not really," he said.

She had been hoping for a speedy resolution so that life could get back to normal. She was probably foolish to think that there could be a simple answer.

"You were okay here last night?"

"Fine. Everything went according to plan."

"Good."

Jeremiah opened the driver's side rear door. "I made a lot of deviled eggs," he warned as he pulled out one tray and handed it to her.

"Great, I love them. They're also excellent for throwing at people," she warned.

"Not mine. They're too tasty to throw," he said with a smile. "Can you handle the other tray while I get Captain?"

"Sure," she said, ducking her head slightly so she could see the big German Shepherd seatbelted into the passenger front seat.

She carried the trays of deviled eggs into the house and put them down on the counter near the fruit salad. She walked back into the living room just as Jeremiah was urging Captain out into the backyard to play with Buster.

Traci quickly introduced Jeremiah to her sister and brother-in-law who had wandered back in from the kitchen.

Mark appeared a moment later from the kitchen, drying his hands on a dishtowel. "The gang's all here," he announced.

"Geanie and Joseph aren't," Cindy said.

"Ah, but they are. They're just finding a place to park."

"I'll go see if they need any help bringing in food," Cindy volunteered as she headed out the front door.

Jeremiah followed right behind her. Out front Joseph had parked and was out of the car, Clarice was already straining at her leash, eager to see what other dogs might be there.

"The pooch party is already happening in the backyard," Cindy told him.

"Thanks, I'll be back in a moment to grab the fireworks."

"Don't worry, we've got them," Jeremiah said.

"They're on the backseat and also in the trunk," Joseph said.

"Joseph bought an absolutely obscene amount of fireworks," Geanie said with a pleased grin.

"In my defense Mark said to bring as much as I wanted," Joseph called over his shoulder just before disappearing into the house.

45

"Famous last words," Cindy said with a grin.

"Are you sure you guys have this?" Geanie asked. "I need to go put this cake in the refrigerator but I can come right back."

"Go, relax," Cindy said. "We've got this."

Jeremiah opened the door to the backseat, then popped the trunk and whistled. "This is quite a lot, really."

Cindy glanced around and saw the trunk filled to bursting. She whistled low. "We're certainly going to light up the sky," she said. "Do you think-"

She looked up and stopped talking. Jeremiah was turned, facing down the street, his shoulders tensed, his jaw clamped, and his hands balled into fists at his side. She turned to see what he was staring at and her heart began to pound. There, just a few houses down, a man stood on the sidewalk. He was wearing a dark trenchcoat and sunglasses. A shiver slid up her spine. There was something about him that she found instantly intimidating.

"Who is that?" she whispered.

"No one you want to know," Jeremiah said, voice low. "Stay here."

She nodded and Jeremiah walked down the street, his stride long, purposeful. The other man waited, unflinching. A sick feeling twisted in her stomach.

Jeremiah didn't like anything about this situation, least of all that it was so highly public. He walked quickly and a moment later was standing in front of the man in the coat.

"What do you want?" he growled.

"Much," the other man replied.

Jeremiah's fears were coming true.

"I have nothing to give."

"On the contrary, you might have more to give than any of the rest of us, *malakh ha-mavet.*"

5

"That's not who I am, not anymore," Jeremiah said, shaking his head.

"There is no shame in being the angel of death. How many thousands, how many tens of thousands of lives have you saved through that work?"

"That number is not for us to know. Only G-d can answer that. Look, walk away and I will forget about your visit," Jeremiah said.

"That is not for me to decide. And if something were to happen to me our masters would just send others. You are needed in Israel."

"I've heard that I am not the only one."

"I have heard this as well. I do not know. I have been sent to retrieve you. That is all I know. They have not told me why, but those they are calling back, the skills and knowledge that they possess are essential. My friend, this must be important. Perhaps the most important assignment any of us has ever had."

Jeremiah felt sick just pondering what that might be. "When do we have to leave?"

"There is a plane tonight. You will have a couple of hours to gather some clothes, say goodbye to a few friends. Just in case."

"I'm surprised I'm being allowed."

"My superiors. They do not know that I will have approached you early. I felt, given who you were, that some courtesy was in order, rabbi."

"Did you have anything to do with putting an envelope with malakh ha-mavet written on it in that woman's car yesterday?" he said, inclining his head toward Cindy who was standing next to Joseph's car, watching them intently.

The other man frowned. "I would not have done this. I arrived only two hours ago and have come to you from the airport. Such things should not be written, nor used to frighten our women."

Jeremiah didn't bother explaining that Cindy wasn't his woman. The more he denied it the more strongly the other man would believe it.

"Where shall I meet you?"

The other man shook his head. "I am respectful, not stupid. I know you do not wish to go with me. I understand this. So, I will stay with you."

Jeremiah glanced at Mark's house. "My friends aren't expecting me to bring someone else."

"You can tell them I am your cousin, Aaron, here on business and stopped in for a surprise visit. How could they turn me away?"

Aaron hadn't left the note in Cindy's car. That meant that it was almost certainly one of the men who wanted him dead who had done it. He couldn't leave her alone and without protection.

"I need to make a call."

"By all means. Then we can see your friends."

Jeremiah paced a few steps away. He pulled out his phone and dialed the number that Martin, the C.I.A. agent, had given him in Vegas. He had committed that number to memory in case he would ever need it.

The phone rang twice before Martin answered. "Go," the man said, voice tense.

"It's Rabbi Silverman. I need a favor."

"Rabbi, I wish I could help, but this is not a good time. In five minutes I'm boarding a plane for Israel."

"You're being reassigned there?"

"For the moment it seems."

"Why?"

"No one's saying, but it can't be good."

"Why you?"

"I spent some time in the country a few years back. Apparently my expertise is required."

"I'll be heading back there myself in a few hours," Jeremiah admitted.

"Maybe I'll see you there. My gut is telling me that something very bad is about to go down. Gotta go."

Martin ended the call and Jeremiah felt his own stomach twist even more. He also had a feeling something very bad was about to happen.

He turned back to Aaron. It was as good a name to call the man as any. His mind was racing as he worried about Cindy and what could happen to her here while he was in Israel. If the men after him found him suddenly gone they might take their frustrations out on her. He had to figure out something to protect her.

"Let's go to the party, cousin."

Jeremiah walked toward Cindy with Aaron a step behind him. Cindy was standing, arms folded over her chest, face pale but resolute. She could sense that something was wrong.

"Cindy, this is my cousin, Aaron. He's here on business but had the day off and thought he'd surprise me."

"It's an honor to meet you," Aaron said.

Cindy glared, clearly not believing it for a minute. "Who is he really?"

Jeremiah stepped closer to her so their bodies were practically touching. "Not now," he said, dropping his voice low.

She nodded slowly, clearly not happy but willing to wait for an explanation. She looked at Aaron. "Help me carry these fireworks into the house."

"Yes," he said, hastening to grab an armful of boxes each stuffed with dozens of different fireworks.

Jeremiah grabbed more from the trunk and Cindy scooped up the ones on the backseat. Together the three of them trooped inside and out to the back where they deposited them on a round concrete slab that looked like it could have been used for a gazebo or above ground pool.

"I'll get the last of them," Cindy said. "You should introduce your cousin around."

"Thank you," Jeremiah said.

By the time she had returned he had introduced Aaron to everyone present. Only Mark seemed suspicious of Aaron's sudden appearance. Captain came over and sniffed Aaron then went back to playing with the other dogs. It was proof that it hadn't been Aaron's scent on the envelope, which was actually bad news because it confirmed his fears about who had been behind it.

Mark had fired up the grill and was getting ready to put burgers and hot dogs on. Cindy began bringing food outside and Doug and Liam rushed to help her. Jeremiah sat down at one of the tables, trying to figure out what his options were.

Traci sat down nearby next to her sister Amber.

"So, what are you going to name the baby?" Amber asked.

"Well, we don't know yet if it's a boy or a girl," Traci said.

She was lying. Jeremiah could hear it in her voice and see it in her eyes. There were little tells that wouldn't have been noticeable to most people. He wasn't most people, though, and he was in a state of hyperawareness at the moment.

"I understand that, but surely there've been some names you've been thinking about," Amber pushed.

"Well, we like Crystal, Rachel, or Kylie for girl names. We're having a bit more of a problem agreeing on boy names we both like. Although, I was actually starting to think that Jeremiah would be a nice name." Traci flashed him a smile.

Jeremiah frowned. "I'm flattered, but in Jewish culture we don't name babies after people who are living. So, unless you know something that I don't know..."

He saw Mark bite his lip, clearly trying to contain a comment.

Then again, if things went south naming the baby after him might not be a problem at all.

"Oh, I know! What about Chuck? You know I saw Chuck Norris-"

"At an airport once, we know," Mark said with a groan.

"We're not naming the baby Chuck," Traci said.

"But Chuck Norris is awesome," Amber said.

"Granted, but I still am not naming my baby Chuck," Traci said firmly.

"What about Kyle? That's a nice name."

"No!" Mark, Traci, Cindy and Jeremiah all said at exactly the same moment.

"Overreact much?" Amber asked as Traci broke into giggles.

"Trust us, we were not overreacting at all," Mark said.

It was funny and Jeremiah wished he could laugh, but he was lucky to barely manage a smile. Cindy was also on edge. Fortunately no one else seemed to notice. For his part Aaron was laughing and chatting amicably with everyone as though he didn't have a care in the world. It was easy for him. His whole life wasn't being destroyed.

When the food was ready Jeremiah ate two hamburgers. He barely tasted them, but everyone else went out of their way to say how delicious they were. Mark beamed with pride. Jeremiah ate some of the side dishes, but couldn't have said a word about how they tasted either.

While he had temporarily lost his sense of taste, his hearing and vision had grown quite acute, and he found himself jumping at sounds such as the sudden barking of one of the dogs.

Once he had finished eating, Jeremiah had finally come to a decision and it wasn't an easy one. While people began clearing away the food Jeremiah approached Mark.

"Can we talk for a minute, alone?"

"Sure," Mark said looking a bit apprehensive. "Let's go to my office."

They walked into the house and a moment later they were sitting down in Mark's office with the door closed. The windows looked out onto the yard. Mercifully Aaron hadn't insisted on following. From where he was sitting he could easily see Jeremiah in the office so he would know that he wasn't running.

"What's up?" Mark asked as he leaned back in his desk chair.

"You know how yesterday you said that someday we were going to have to talk about those things that we don't talk about?"

"Yeah."

"Well, someday is today."

Mark swore and leaned suddenly forward in his chair. "Something's happened."

"I'm afraid it has," Jeremiah said. "I had hoped to never have to say what I'm about to say to you, but I'm fresh out of options."

Jeremiah took a deep breath. "As you've guessed I was a different man before I came here. The truth is that before I was forced into retirement I worked for the Mossad."

Mark whistled low. "I knew it had to be something like that. Does Cindy know?"

"I had to tell her a few months back, right after Geanie and Joseph's wedding."

"Had to tell her?"

"I had inadvertently put her in danger and she needed to understand what was happening."

"How had you put her in danger?"

"You know the dead man at the church during the wedding, the one you found me with?"

"I remember."

"I killed him. He wasn't part of the plot to kill Geanie. He was after me and he was trying to kill Cindy to get to me."

54

Mark passed a hand over his face. "Why are you telling me this? You're confessing to killing the man."

"I'm telling my friend what we're up against."

"I don't follow."

"The man had friends, others who hated me and are targeting me because of my old life. One of them left an envelope in Cindy's car yesterday, a reminder that they're coming after me and they haven't forgotten."

"Who are these people?"

"Terrorists. I know that much. Beyond that, though, I don't know anything. I'm not even sure where their vendetta against me personally comes from."

"Oh, swell. So, that's why you had Cindy spend the night at our house last night."

"Yes, and why I'm going to need your help even more now than ever."

"You seem like you're able to take care of yourself and Cindy."

"Normally I would agree with you," Jeremiah said with a sigh. "But, as of tonight, I won't be here to take care of Cindy."

"Why, where are you going?"

"My cousin Aaron out there. He's not my cousin. He was sent to bring me back to Israel. I'm being reactivated, brought out of retirement for something and whatever it is it has to be very bad."

Mark swore under his breath. He pressed a hand to his forehead. "How long will you be gone?"

"I don't know."

Mark paused and stared out the window for a moment, clearly trying to take everything in. Finally he turned back. "I guess the real question is, will you be back?"

"If it's within my power to do so I will come back."

"You mean, if you're not dead," Mark said bluntly.

Jeremiah nodded.

"This is a helluva bomb to drop on a guy," Mark said.

"I'm sorry."

Mark shook his head. "I always knew there was something about you. You know just yesterday I was stressing out about it, about not wanting to jump to conclusions or accuse you of things I had no proof of."

"What things?" Jeremiah asked sharply.

"Well, for one, the murder of that homeless guy, the one who turned up on your lawn. I found out yesterday that he was a possible witness in a murder that happened a few months before his. It's a cold case now. Iranian student killed, no rhyme or reason or suspects. Yet strangely one of the few possible witnesses ends up killed himself, and on your lawn."

Jeremiah leaned forward intently. "Are you sure he witnessed this student's murder?"

"Reasonably."

"Then whoever killed him might be the same people who killed the student."

"Seems reasonable. Of course, then I'm asking myself how you somehow end up in the middle of all that."

"I don't know anything about an Iranian student. However, the homeless man I saw in the park not that long before he was killed. He recognized me and ran."

"Recognized you from where?"

"From the old days. He used to work for the C.I.A."

Mark swore again.

"And the only place we saw each other before that day in the park was in Iran. I also believe that the men who killed him are the same ones coming after me and Cindy."

Mark passed a hand over his face. "Why go after the homeless guy? Because they figured out he had a connection to you?"

"I don't know. I don't even know why the guy was apparently headed to my house when he got killed. It's especially confusing since he ran away from me at the park."

"Maybe he had some information that he needed to share that he didn't want to trust to the police," Mark speculated.

"You mean about the Iranian kid and who killed him and why?"

"Could be. If his murder was anything more than a random act or a personal hatred it could have had some other cause."

"Like a political one?" Jeremiah asked.

"Or something. So, maybe what we should be asking is what the student was involved in or witnessed that could have gotten him killed."

"I have a terrible feeling that it's all interconnected somehow," Jeremiah said.

"You and me both," Mark said, standing up and beginning to pace the room. "We just have to figure out how."

"I'm afraid you'll have to work on that without me," Jeremiah said grimly.

"What do you need me to do?"

"Protect Cindy as best you can. When they learn that I'm gone they might try to retaliate or try and draw me out."

"Do you know what you're asking of me?"

"I do. I'm asking you to risk your own family's safety to help her, to help me. It's a terrible burden."

"But one I'll bear as long as I can," Mark said.

"I appreciate that."

Jeremiah stood. Time was running out and he needed to talk to Cindy before he had to go. He was leaving a nightmare behind him and putting those he cared about in the line of fire. He wished he had some other choice. He stretched out his hand and without hesitation Mark shook it.

"You're a good man, detective."

"And you're a bad man, rabbi."

Jeremiah gave him a sad smile. "More than you know."

"I suspect you'll be wanting to talk to Cindy alone."

"That would be preferable."

"Then stay here. I'll send her in."

"Thanks," Jeremiah said, sitting back down.

When Mark emerged from the house without Jeremiah Cindy felt her heart begin to race. Something was happening, something bad. She could feel it. She intercepted Mark before he made it back to a table.

"What is going on? you have to tell me," she said, keeping her voice low.

He gave her the strangest look and then put his hand on her shoulder. "Jeremiah's in my office. He needs to talk to you." He squeezed her shoulder. "We're here for you. Whatever you need."

For a moment she could swear she saw tears in his eyes. He turned away quickly, though, and headed over to Traci. Dread filled Cindy and her feet felt like they were made of lead as she forced herself forward one step at a time.

She was right. Things were bad. Worse than she'd feared.

A minute later she was inside Mark's office. Her hands were shaking as she sat down in a chair and stared expectantly at Jeremiah. He stared at her like he was trying to memorize her face.

Finally she cleared her throat. "Mark said you wanted to talk to me."

Jeremiah nodded.

"This has something to do with that guy Aaron who isn't your cousin, doesn't it?"

"Yes."

"Is he one of the ones who's trying to hurt you?"

"No, he isn't. But he was sent to bring me back to Israel. I've been recalled, reactivated as a Mossad agent."

"What?" Cindy gasped. Something like that had never even crossed her mind. "They can do that?"

"They can and they have. I don't know what's going on, but it's something big, something important or they wouldn't be dragging me out of retirement."

"But you are retired. You have been for a while. Don't they have other people who can do what you did?"

Jeremiah grimaced. "Maybe, maybe not. I was especially good at what I did. They might need me for some other reason, my experience, expertise, contacts. I don't know and I won't know anything more until I get there."

"When do you leave?"

"In just a couple of hours."

"Will you come back?" she asked.

The question hung in the air between them. He started to say something, then stopped. He dropped his eyes. "I'll try," he whispered.

"That's not good enough." She jumped to her feet, fear galvanizing her. "I'm not going to lose you, not like this. And I'm not going to spend weeks or months or even years wondering if you're dead or alive. I'm not going to spend that time waiting for one of your enemies to finally come for me either."

"Cindy, you have to understand-"

"No! I don't have to understand."

She felt like she was on fire and yet freezing to death at the same time. Waves of heat and cold chased each other through her body. She felt like her brain was whirling faster and faster and she couldn't put her thoughts together in any way that made sense. All she knew was that if she didn't do something she would probably never see Jeremiah again.

She stormed out of Mark's office and headed for the backyard. She felt Jeremiah grab her arm, but she yanked free. She hit the backyard and made her way straight to Aaron who was playing with Captain.

The man looked up, saw her, and quickly stood. The smile disappeared from his face.

"Cindy, stop!" she heard Jeremiah as though he was a long distance away. She felt his hand descend on her shoulder, but she continued forward.

60

"You!" she hissed as she came to a stop in front of Aaron.

His eyes narrowed and he glanced over her shoulder, probably at Jeremiah, and then looked back at her.

"Is there a problem?" he asked.

"A huge one. Jeremiah isn't going anywhere. He's needed here. His congregation needs him. His friends need him. I need him. There are terrorists around who are just waiting for an opportunity to strike at us, and I'm not going to let him go off to Israel and get himself killed over something that I won't even know what it is."

"I haven't been told why-"

"Even if you had it wouldn't make any difference. I'm not letting Jeremiah out of my sight. Every time I do, bad things happen, and I refuse to be here sick with grief and worry waiting for some terrorist to kill me to get at him."

"I'm sure your friend the detective can help keep you safe."

"No one can keep me safe except for Jeremiah. And you know what? He needs me just as much as I need him."

Aaron shrugged his shoulders. "I am sorry, but there is nothing I can do. Jeremiah must return with me to Israel."

Cindy was shaking now, fury and terror flooding through her. She stared at him dead in the eyes. "Then I'm going, too."

6

Mark gaped at Cindy. Everything was going sideways and spinning dangerously out of control. However this ended it wasn't going to be pretty.

"Liam, Traci, get everyone else inside the house," Mark ordered. Whatever was about to happen they needed to eliminate the wildcards from the equation.

"Okay, inside everyone," Traci called, her voice trembling slightly as she got up.

There was shocked silence, but everyone followed her inside. Liam was the last in and he shut the sliding glass door behind him. Mark wished he was in there with them, but this was his house and the safety of the people there was his responsibility. Mark moved to join the trio who were all showing varying degrees of agitation.

"Cindy, what you're asking is impossible," Jeremiah said, his voice low, agitated, and his accent suddenly much, much thicker.

"Listen to Jeremiah. He knows what's best," Aaron said.

"Not right now he doesn't. What's best is for me to stick to him like glue. We always do our best work when helping each other."

"Cindy, what I've got to do you can't help me with."

"You don't know that," Mark interjected. Jeremiah glared at him, but he continued. "You told me you have no idea what the mission is or why they need you. So, you really have no way of knowing that Cindy can't help you, be an extra pair of eyes, another mind to bounce things off of."

Jeremiah shook his head. "You have no idea what things will be like there."

"People will probably be trying to kill her. As opposed to here where people will definitely be trying to kill her," Mark said, crossing his arms over his chest.

Jeremiah was angry, any fool could see that. He was also scared. Normally Mark would have backed away with his hands in the air, but these were extraordinary circumstances.

"I'm not taking Cindy with me," Jeremiah said. "It's too dangerous."

Cindy crossed her arms over her chest and glared daggers at Jeremiah and Aaron. "I'm guessing it won't be nearly as dangerous as what happens if you don't take me with you."

"And what would that be?" Aaron asked.

"I'll fly to Israel by myself and search for you."

"That is ridiculous, you would never find him," Aaron argued.

"No, but I bet I'd find plenty of danger."

Jeremiah flinched. Mark could tell that Cindy meant every word she was saying and the rabbi could tell, too.

"You hate danger," Jeremiah whispered.

"Not as much as I hate the thought of losing you."

Jeremiah reached out and pulled Cindy into a fierce hug. "No matter what I choose you won't be safe," Mark could hear him whisper.

Cindy didn't say anything.

Mark looked at Aaron. "I'm guessing little things like getting a visa won't be a problem," he said somewhat sarcastically.

"For travel between our countries a visa can be obtained at the point of entry on arrival in Israel," Aaron answered. "But to answer your question, it won't be a problem. Obviously, though, I cannot guarantee her safety."

Mark nodded as he tried hard to swallow around the sudden lump in his throat. He knew that he might never see either of them again, and even though he dealt with death and bereaved loved ones daily in his job it was still hard to imagine his loved ones being killed.

When Jeremiah and Cindy finally broke apart Mark made eye contact with the rabbi. "I'll continue to work on things here from my end. The murders we discussed. If I find anything interesting I'll call you."

"Thank you, my friend," Jeremiah said.

Mark shook his hand. "Just make sure to let us know you're okay."

Jeremiah nodded.

Mark turned and hugged Cindy, struggling to hold back tears. "Watch out for each other, okay?"

She nodded.

"It's a different world over there, an entirely different culture. You do everything Jeremiah tells you, too, okay?"

"I will," she promised, her voice quavering.

Mark stepped back and wiped the back of his hand across his eyes. "Is there anything you need me to do?"

"If you could look after Captain, I'd appreciate it," Jeremiah said.

"Done. Buster loves having company."

"And if you could tell Marie that my cousin called...a family emergency...and I had to fly back to Israel. Tell her to get a substitute rabbi for at least three or four weeks, just to be safe."

"I can do that. Should I tell the church something similar for you?" Mark asked, addressing Cindy.

She nodded.

"Alright, consider it done. Now get out of here, all of you, before someone makes a scene," he said.

The three of them looked at each other and then turned and walked into the house. Mark stood for a moment, trying to gather himself together before following behind.

Cindy felt like she was walking through a dream. Nothing felt quite real to her. She was still coming to terms with what she'd just said and done and what it all meant. Israel. She was going to Israel with Jeremiah. She'd daydreamed before about being able to see the Holy Land with him as her guide, but what they were walking into was more of a nightmare. There was every chance that they were going to die and that terrified her. What terrified her more, though, was the thought of staying behind and having to keep on living if Jeremiah died.

All kinds of thoughts kept smashing together in her head. Maybe Traci was right about everything. Maybe Cindy needed to tell Jeremiah how she felt. Then again, she might have just done that. She was a little fuzzy on what all she had actually said.

Inside the house strained faces turned toward them. Everyone knew something was wrong. They just didn't know what was wrong. Maybe it was better that way. Maybe not. She'd let Mark sort it out once they were gone.

The first person she saw was Geanie and she threw her arms around her and hugged her close. "Be safe," Cindy whispered to her. After all, someone should be.

She let go of her and turned to find Traci standing, fear shimmering in the tears in her eyes. "It's going to be okay," she whispered to Traci as she hugged her, even though she knew that might be a lie.

At last Cindy saw Joseph. In some ways she was going to miss him most of all. He'd been one of her first, true close friends. She hugged him tight. "Take care of everyone for me," she whispered.

"Take care of yourself," he whispered back.

She nodded as she stepped back. She turned toward the door and saw Mark standing there. Tears were shining in his eyes. She walked up to him.

"Are you sure you want to do this?" he asked, voice so low only she could hear.

"Yes."

She started to hug him and then pulled back. "I'm sorry," she said, tears beginning to spill down her cheeks.

"I understand," he said, tears flowing freely from his eyes as well. She pulled her keys out of her purse. "Here, to the car and the house. Geanie still has a set of house keys, too."

Mark took them with a nod. Jeremiah handed over his keys as well.

Cindy was feeling dizzy as they walked out the front door. A small voice inside her head said it wasn't too late to change her mind. She could stay and do the smart thing. She did her best to shut that voice out. For better or for worse she had committed herself to this and she would see it through.

Jeremiah wrapped his hand around hers, startling her. When he squeezed her hand she squeezed back. Slowly her head began to clear. Whatever happened now, at least they were in it together.

Aaron had a rental car and Cindy got into the backseat, expecting Jeremiah to sit up front with Aaron. To her surprise he climbed in the back with her. He picked up her hand again and held it tight.

They made it to Jeremiah's house and she watched in awe as he picked the lock on his front door in seconds. Inside he moved swiftly, gathering up the things he needed for the trip. Fifteen minutes later he was closing the door with a look of sorrow on his face.

A few minutes later they made it to Cindy's house. She hadn't even thought about needing to go there and pack when she gave Mark her key. She assumed Jeremiah would pick that lock, too, but he surprised her by producing a key.

"Where did you get that?"

"I've had this since the day after you moved into this house," he said. "You never know when a thing like this will be useful."

Inside the house she turned to him. "I don't know what types of clothes I should pack," she admitted.

"I'll pack clothes for you. You get together your toiletries, undergarments, and anything else you might need. Deal?"

She nodded. She grabbed a suitcase out of her closet and handed it to him then got herself a small bag and headed into the bathroom. Five minutes later she handed him the bag of toiletries to put in the suitcase. She opened her underwear drawer, scooped up what she could and shoved it into the suitcase. Flushing, she moved one of the shirts he'd already packed to cover them.

Next Cindy went into her office and got her passport out of the small safe she kept her valuable documents in. She had renewed it several months before in case she did get an opportunity to go to Israel someday. It was a good thing she had.

Hurry, hurry, hurry. It was like a drumbeat pounding in her head. Once she'd gotten everything she could think of she walked around the house, looking at everything. It struck her after a moment that what she was actually doing was saying goodbye. She might not make it back, and if she did, odds were she would be changed and seeing everything with different eyes.

She hadn't told Mark to say anything to her parents or Kyle. It was best this way. If she came back they would have spent the time needlessly worrying and they'd have questions she wouldn't want to answer. If she didn't...she trusted Geanie would say something to them when the time was right.

A minute later Jeremiah joined her in the living room, carrying her suitcase. She looked at him and then gestured around her. "Not much to show for a life," she said.

He squeezed her shoulder with his free hand. "Actually, it's quite a lot. Besides, this isn't the end. It's only the beginning of a new chapter."

She prayed that he was right.

She turned and followed him out of the house, watching numbly as he locked the door. Aaron was waiting at the car and he took the bag from Jeremiah. She was appreciative of the fact that he'd stayed outside instead of invading her home.

She climbed back in the backseat, grateful that Jeremiah did as well. He held her hand the entire drive to the airport which seemed to take a lifetime.

They moved through the airport quickly and efficiently. She stuck as close to Jeremiah as she could, trusting him to take care of everything while she still tried to come to terms with what was happening. Once they made it to the gate the three of them sat together somewhat separated from the other passengers.

She noticed that Jeremiah's eyes were constantly moving, sweeping over the other passengers, people walking by, everyone and everything. It was the same with Aaron.

"We'll be landing in New Jersey and changing planes there. Then it's straight to Tel Aviv," Jeremiah said quietly without looking at her.

"Okay," she said. "Is there anything I need to do?"

"Get some rest if you can. They'll be long flights and who knows what's waiting for us on the other end."

That wasn't reassuring but it was good advice. She leaned back in her chair and closed her eyes, trying to calm herself down. It would be a start if she could at least unclench her fists.

After what seemed a very short time Jeremiah touched her arm. "They're boarding our flight," he said.

She had managed to tune out all the announcements that kept playing so she hadn't realized it was time. She stood quickly, feeling nervous.

They boarded the plane and sat together with Jeremiah in the middle and Cindy in the window seat. She couldn't help but feel like Aaron was sitting on the end to make sure they didn't go anywhere. It was a plane, though. There was nowhere for them to run.

She dozed fitfully, having no interest in the movie that was playing. At last they touched down in New Jersey and again she found herself hovering next to Jeremiah as they made their way to the next gate.

Half an hour later she was sitting down on the second plane, the last one. If she closed her eyes to sleep when she opened them she'd be in Israel. Jeremiah squeezed her hand as though sensing her trepidation. They were in this together and that gave her courage. She had insisted on coming, she couldn't slow him down. She had to be strong, careful, and do what he asked. She made a vow as she sat there in that plane seat as the wheels left the ground and they headed for Tel Aviv. No matter what happened they would survive and both of them would go home to California, together.

"Have you been back, since..." she asked, letting the question drift off because she was pretty sure she already knew the answer.

"No."

Jeremiah leaned his head back against the headrest and closed his eyes. A few minutes later his breathing slowed. He was asleep. That was good. She should probably try to sleep as well. It was dark outside and all the shades were down. The cabin lights were off and a couple of reading lights burned in the darkness.

She tilted her head back and tried to relax. She focused on the sound of the engines that were near her seat. As the plane leveled off she could hear people around the cabin beginning to snore. At least some people were getting to rest.

On the aisle Aaron shifted slightly in his seat then seemed to settle down. She wished she could. Jeremiah was sleeping away and she was going to be awake the entire flight, she could feel it. She wondered how soon before the flight attendants initiated a beverage service. Maybe she could get some hot tea to soothe her nerves.

Perhaps she could just hit the call button now and someone would be nice enough to get her the tea so she wouldn't have to wait. She opened her eyes. She had her head tilted toward Jeremiah and Aaron. She expected them to both be asleep. Jeremiah was, but Aaron was awake and doing something with his hands. A moment later she saw that he was holding a needle and it was hovering over Jeremiah's arm.

7

With a cry Cindy lunged forward and grabbed Aaron's wrist, twisting it hard so that the syringe pointed toward him instead of Jeremiah. He grabbed her hand with his free one and tried to pry up her fingers. She held on desperately, trying to stand to get more leverage, but was thwarted by her seatbelt.

As he began to twist his hand back she frantically felt for the seatbelt release with her left. He was stronger than she was and she was losing ground. Just as the needle came within a hair's breadth of Jeremiah's leg her index finger caught the release. She yanked up on it, and her seatbelt released.

Cindy lunged to her feet, threw her body halfway across Jeremiah, and jabbed three of her fingers as hard as she could into Aaron's throat right at his Adam's apple. He gasped and let go of her hand to grab for his throat. Throwing her body weight behind her arm she was able to twist his hand with the syringe back toward him.

She fell further onto Jeremiah who stirred for the first time during the struggle. Suddenly his hand reached out, locked over Aaron's hand and he managed to shove the needle into Aaron's leg. Jeremiah depressed the plunger. Aaron was still gasping and choking, eyes bugging out of his head.

Jeremiah gently pushed Cindy back in the direction of her seat and she fell back into it, smacking her elbow hard on the arm rest. Jeremiah clamped his right hand over Aaron's mouth and with his left removed the syringe. He leaned down and when he straightened he no longer had the needle.

A few seconds later Aaron's entire body went lax. Jeremiah removed his hand from Aaron's mouth and closed the man's eyes. He leaned back in his chair just as a flight attendant appeared.

"Is there a problem?" the woman asked, her voice tense.

"I am so sorry," Jeremiah said. "I was having a terrible nightmare and I'm afraid I might have been thrashing around a bit. Fortunately my wife was able to wake me," he said, grabbing Cindy's hand.

The woman's eyes drifted to Aaron.

"My cousin usually sleeps like the dead. He's afraid of flying so his doctor gave him something to relax him. I don't think he'll be waking up any time soon."

The woman nodded slowly. "Okay. Is there anything I can get you?"

"No, we're sorry if we were any bother," Jeremiah said.

The woman took another look at Aaron, then turned and walked back down the aisle.

Cindy slumped in momentary relief as some of the adrenalin started to drain from her body. They weren't out of the woods yet, though. Not by any means. Jeremiah turned to look at her. His eyes were a little glazed.

She leaned close so she could whisper softly in his ear. She didn't need anyone overhearing. "Is he dead?"

She pulled back slightly and Jeremiah nodded.

She leaned back in. "Are you okay? You don't look right."

He twisted his head and she turned so he could whisper to her. "I think he drugged my water in the terminal. I'm still feeling the effects. You saved my life. Thank you."

"You're welcome. What do we do now?" she whispered back.

"Wait until we land then get off this plane before they realize what's happened."

"Why did...they...want to kill you?"

"I don't know. They might not have had anything to do with it."

"Are we going to Israel for nothing?"

"We'll see."

Cindy wanted to keep talking but twisting to whisper to Jeremiah kept bringing Aaron's face into her line of sight. And she didn't want to look at the man who had almost killed Jeremiah.

She leaned her head back against the headrest. There was no way she was sleeping now, not with all the thoughts whirling through her head. She was trying not to think about what was going to happen when they landed. What if Aaron's death was discovered before they could disembark? What if there were people waiting on the other end who would kill her and Jeremiah on sight?

She wondered what Aaron had planned to do to her once Jeremiah was dead. She shuddered at the thought. He probably would have killed her too. She should have been suspicious that he didn't fight too hard against the idea of her coming along. Maybe he was counting on her keeping Jeremiah distracted which would only make killing him easier.

She felt like she was going to be sick. She had no idea what was going to happen when they landed. All she did know was that her only chance of survival was sticking to Jeremiah like glue.

Jeremiah was still struggling to fight off the effects of whatever sedative Aaron had slipped him. It had been Cindy thrashing around on top of him that had brought him to. If she hadn't insisted on coming along he would be dead. And likely no one back home in California would ever have known what had become of him. Cindy would have spent her life wondering if he was dead or alive.

He shook his head. He owed her his life. That was a tremendous thing. He had saved her life plenty of times, but this was the first time he had incontrovertible proof that without her he would have been killed.

From now on he was going to have to be extremely vigilant to ensure her safety as well as his own. Where they were going he couldn't afford a single slipup or miscalculation.

He started going over every interaction with the dead man next to him, trying to determine who might have sent Aaron to kill him. It didn't make sense that the Mossad would want him dead, not after they'd gone through all the trouble to retire and relocate him. Besides, enough time had passed he would have fallen off the radar. Unless killing the terrorist at the wedding had put him right back on it.

That single act had certainly got the C.I.A.'s attention and it stood to reason the Mossad would have noticed as well. They could have let a few months lapse so Jeremiah's death wouldn't be quickly connected to the other one. But why try to kill him on the plane?

Aaron had had at least half a dozen chances to kill him before that. Maybe he didn't care to take a chance on Jeremiah being able to respond and fight back. Or maybe whoever had ordered Aaron to kill him wanted Jeremiah's body in Israel for some reason. Proof of death perhaps?

He was sure of one thing. Aaron hadn't been working alone. If he had been coming after Jeremiah on his own for some reason he would have gone about things completely different. Aaron would have either killed him back in California at some point when Jeremiah wasn't expecting it. Or he would have captured him, explained what he was getting revenge for, and then he would have killed Jeremiah.

Jeremiah had been suspicious that Aaron was giving him time to say goodbye to his friends. He had decided, though, that it had been a simple act of kindness and respect that was permissible because of the time for their flight. It also hadn't made sense that Aaron caved so easily on letting Cindy come with them. But Jeremiah knew that for particularly valuable assets occasionally things like that were allowed to ensure their willing cooperation.

So, the big question remained. Was he a valuable asset, a dangerous liability, or something else entirely? Since there was no way to know the answer until they walked off the plane in Tel Aviv he was going to have to be ready for anything. To that end he began running scenarios in his mind trying to work out a plan for every possible contingency. When they landed at the airport he wanted to be ready for anything and everything. Their lives would likely depend on it.

It was midnight and Mark couldn't sleep. Instead he was up pacing in the family room. Buster had followed him from the bedroom, but once he realized that there was nothing interesting going on he returned. Captain was stretched out next to the front door, half asleep, clearly hoping Jeremiah was coming back soon. His eyes were following Mark as he walked back and forth.

Everything was topsy turvy. He had always known there was something up with Jeremiah. He was used to having those suspicions. For once, though, having a mystery solved didn't make him feel any better. For some reason he felt worse and it was driving him crazy.

Maybe it was because he had a very bad feeling about whatever it was that Jeremiah and Cindy were getting into. Rationally he realized that he probably didn't have to worry too much about Jeremiah. The rabbi knew how to handle himself in just about any situation. That was probably one of the things that had made him a good Mossad agent. Still, he was worried about him. Even the most talented in any field could have an off day or be completely blindsided by something.

As much as he was worried about Jeremiah he was ten times more worried about Cindy. She had come a long way from that withdrawn, terrified woman he had first met a couple of years ago. She was practically a different person these days. Yet despite all that, and all the things she had survived in those couple years, this was totally different. She'd be in a foreign country, one that was pretty much always a war zone, cut off from everyone that might be able to help her. Add to that whatever super bad, terrifying crap that was enough for the Mossad to reactivate Jeremiah and you had a recipe for disaster.

"Worrying yourself sick isn't going to help them."

Mark jumped and turned with a shout. Traci stared at him with wide, startled eyes.

"You scared me," he told her.

"Apparently. Couldn't sleep?"

"No."

"I'm worried, too," she said, sitting down on the couch.

She looked tired and he felt guilty for interrupting her sleep.

"I'm sorry for waking you."

"You didn't. I couldn't get comfortable. I'm having some painful gas. I'm not sure if the food didn't agree with me or if it was all the excitement."

"There was a lot of excitement, that's for sure. Too much."

"What do you think the Mossad wants with Jeremiah?" Traci asked.

Of course he'd told her the truth about what was going on. There was no way he was carrying the burden of that knowledge by himself.

"I don't know. It could be he's an expert on a particular thing or person that has suddenly become an issue. Or maybe it's something connected to something he worked on for them."

"Poor Cindy, getting pulled into the middle of this nightmare."

"She didn't have to go," Mark pointed out.

"Yes, she did. She loves him and she's terrified she's going to lose him."

Mark stopped and looked at her. "You love me and you don't follow me off on every police call."

Traci smiled at him. "That's because you're my husband. You know I love you, and I know that you love me and would do everything in your power to fight to come back to me. Cindy doesn't have that reassurance. She's never told Jeremiah how she feels, and she's not positive how he feels. She's terrified that if she let him go he wouldn't come back even if he was alive."

Mark sighed. "Life would be so much simpler if the two of them got married."

"Or if they at least were honest with each other about how they felt."

"When they get back I have half a mind to lock them in a room and not let them out until they tell each other how they feel."

"Might work if Jeremiah doesn't decide to pick the lock instead."

Mark rolled his eyes.

Captain lifted his head and looked over at Traci. The big dog got up and padded over to her, then got up on the couch next to her and laid down.

"I wish there was something we could do to help," Traci said as she petted the dog's head. Captain closed his eyes, clearly enjoying the attention.

"That's part of what's had me up. I keep thinking about this case from a couple of years ago. Do you remember that Iranian student that was murdered? We had zero leads on it. I read something in the file yesterday, though, that got me thinking. I'm wondering if his death was actually linked to some much larger thing, perhaps politically or even globally."

"Mark-"

"No, hear me out. I know it sounds crazy. According to all his friends and teachers there was nothing about this guy that was likely to get him in trouble. He was nice, quiet but friendly, not quiet like I'm about to try and kill a whole bunch of people kind of quiet."

"Mark-"

"I know, but these days you hear someone described as quiet and that kind of thing comes to mind. No, he wasn't a loner. He had friends. People liked him. There was no one that seemed to bear him any ill will which made it hard to figure out a motive let alone a suspect. But, it turns out a homeless guy who witnessed his murder was a former C.I.A. agent who was killed a couple of months later. I was busy trying to connect the homeless guy to those other homeless killings or even to Jeremiah, but I'm thinking his death has nothing to do with them and everything to do with witnessing this kid's murder.

"What if the kid wasn't killed because he'd done something to piss someone off but because he knew something that was dangerous? When I get back to work I'm going to see what I can find out about his family and friends back in Iran. Maybe there are links to terrorism somewhere there. It's possible he was privy, even on accident, to some details of a terrorist plot. Now that would be something someone might kill him over. Don't you think?"

"Mark, I-"

"I know it sounds far-fetched," he said, interrupting her. "But really, in the world we live in stranger things have happened and I'd be remiss if I didn't at least consider the possibility and check out one or two things. Maybe whatever the kid knew he somehow passed on or revealed to the homeless guy. And maybe that's why the homeless guy was on his way to Jeremiah's when he was killed. Maybe his old pals wouldn't believe him anymore because he'd gone a bit off his rocker, but because he recognized Jeremiah from the old days then he was hoping that Jeremiah might actually believe him and still have the connections to do something about it. After all, Jeremiah told me that they knew each other from something that they were both working on in Iran. It has to all fit. It has to be connected. Maybe if I can figure things out on my end it will help Jeremiah and Cindy somehow."

"Mark!"

"Yes, what is it?" he asked, turning to look at her.

She was white as a ghost and she was staring at him with a stricken look on her face.

"What is it?" he asked again, fear starting to race through him.

"We need to go to the hospital. My water just broke."

8

Mark paced in the waiting room, beside himself. He'd driven like a madman to get to the hospital. They hadn't had time to pack anything to take with them. Traci wasn't due to have the baby for two months. Why she was in labor now he didn't know. What was worse was the doctor wouldn't let him back in the room with her. Something had gone horribly wrong, and the longer they left him in the dark the more terrified he became that he was going to lose both his daughter and his wife.

He heard footsteps hurrying down the hall and he turned to face the doorway. A moment later Geanie and Joseph both appeared looking completely haggard.

"We got here as fast as we could," Geanie said, rushing forward to hug him.

He could tell they had. Geanie was wearing mismatched socks and Joseph's hair was sticking out at every possible angle.

"Thank you," he said, choking to get the words out.

"Is there any word?" Joseph asked when Geanie pulled away.

"No. They haven't told me a blasted thing," Mark said. "I'm going crazy here."

"I'll see if I can't pry some information out of someone," Joseph said. He crossed to a chair and pulled out his phone.

Mark stared at him uncomprehendingly. Who did Joseph possibly intend to call to get information?

"Hi, Dan. It's Joseph. I'm calling because I need information on a pregnant patient in the hospital. She's gone into labor two months prematurely and no one is letting us know what's going on with her. Her husband is worried and so am I. Yes. Traci Walters. Okay. Call me back on this number."

Joseph hung up. "We should know something in a minute or two."

"Who was that?" Mark asked.

"The director of the hospital."

Mark blinked. "You know the director?"

"Yes, Dan is our newest Shepherd at the church," Geanie said.

Mark hadn't heard that term in a long time, not since the case where he'd first met everyone. "And that means you can just call him up in the middle of the night for a patient status and he'll give it to you?"

"No, that means he'll take my call in the middle of the night. He'll get us information about Traci because I'm the hospital's largest charitable donor."

Mark nodded. Joseph was rich and he was also connected. If those connections helped Traci or him then he was happy to use them.

A minute later Joseph's phone rang and he quickly answered. "Hello? Yes. They are? Why? Right now? Okay, thanks."

Joseph hung up and he looked pale. Mark felt his stomach clench into knots.

"There have been some complications and they're going to do a C-section. They're taking her into surgery right now."

"I need to see her."

"You can't. She's already sedated and they need to move fast."

Mark sat down next to Joseph who put a hand on his shoulder.

"She's going to be alright. Dan assured me that his finest people are taking care of her. He also instructed them to tell us the moment anything changes."

"I can't believe this is happening," Mark whispered. Traci was his world. If he lost her, he lost everything.

"Did he say what the complications were?" Geanie asked as she sat down.

"No. Just that there were some."

Joseph still had his hand on Mark's left shoulder. Geanie put her hand on his right shoulder and bowed her head. "God, we come before you with troubled hearts. We beg you to guide the doctor's hands and to deliver Traci and the baby safely through this. We pray that you protect them and make this ordeal swift. Afterwards we pray that Traci's recovery is swift. Right now, God, we also pray for Mark. Please ease his pain and fear and give him your peace and the knowledge that everything is going to be okay. We ask all this in Jesus' name. Amen."

"Amen," Joseph echoed.

"Amen," Mark whispered.

"Ladies and gentlemen we will be landing in just a few minutes. Please put your seat backs in the full upright position and put away your trays. Thank you." As soon as the flight attendant had finished speaking the cabin lights flickered on. All around them people were groaning and stretching as they sat up. Shades were raised letting the morning sun stream in.

Next to him Cindy raised her shade. He looked out the window and he could see the earth below them. Israel. He had thought he'd never be stepping foot on her soil again. It was with a mixture of feelings that he saw it now.

Cindy turned to look at him and the fear was plain to read in her eyes. He reached out and grabbed her hand. He squeezed it tight. "It's going to be okay," he said, sounding more confident than he felt. He hesitated then leaned close to her so he could whisper. "Very few people know the name Jeremiah and I'd like to keep it that way," he said.

"What should I call you then?" she asked.

He took a deep breath. He had never thought to speak this name again. "Malachi Abram."

"Is that your real name?"

"The one I was born with, yes," he said.

"Malachi, it sounds like part of the phrase that you said means Angel of Death."

"It should. Malachi and malakh both mean Messenger."

"Which is another word for angel," she said slowly.

He nodded. Not wanting to talk about it any further, he reached down and pretended to adjust his backpack.

A few minutes later the plane touched down. He pulled his backpack out from beneath the seat in front of him. The moment the plane had taxied to the gate Jeremiah stood, climbed over Aaron's body, helped Cindy do the same, and was heading for the front of the plane. Passengers they passed gave them hostile glares. As they neared the front the fasten seatbelt sign was turned off and a couple of people stood up and moved into the aisle in front of them.

"Slicha, eyfoh hasherutim. Excuse me, bathroom emergency," Jeremiah said as he pushed past them, dragging Cindy with him.

Only one person refused to get out of the way and Jeremiah knocked into him hard enough to send him back down into his seat. A moment later they were at the exit to the airplane waiting for the flight attendant to open it.

Finally she did and Jeremiah and Cindy headed up the gangplank quickly, him still holding her hand to ensure that she was right with him. They burst into the waiting room at the gate and Jeremiah swept the space with his eyes, looking for anyone familiar or anyone or anything that looked out of place. Finally his eyes landed on a man in his fifties with dark hair that was silver at his temples. He knew him. The man had been his handler for years.

Jeremiah took a deep breath and walked straight up to him, still clutching Cindy's hand. The man smiled as he approached and stretched out his arms. A moment later he was embracing Jeremiah and kissing him on each cheek.

"Shalom, Malachi."

"Shalom, Solomon."

Solomon turned to eye Cindy.

"Shmah Cindy," Jeremiah told him.

Solomon nodded. Whether he already knew who she was or not he did not give away by his expression.

"Shalom, Cindy," he said solemnly.

"Shalom," she said, her voice tight.

"Yalla, we should go quickly," Jeremiah said.

Solomon turned and led them in the direction of baggage claim. "We were worried about you. We had word two hours ago that the man we sent to get you turned up dead in his hotel room. Aaron was a good man."

"There's a dead man on the plane who claimed to be Aaron then tried to kill me on the flight over."

"I am glad he did not succeed."

"Me, too," Jeremiah said, still looking at everything and everyone around him. It had been a long time since he'd been this hyper-vigilant. His American counterparts had a saying. *Eternal vigilance is the price of liberty.* He had learned long ago that it was also the price of survival.

"We shall take care of this," Solomon said. He pulled a cell phone out of his pocket and made a quick call that Jeremiah could tell was heavily encoded. Finished, he returned the phone to a pocket. "We will know as much as we can about this imposter soon enough."

Solomon's presence combined with what he'd said about the dead agent was proof that the Mossad had been calling him back. That was at least one question resolved. Now he just needed to know why.

Cindy took in everything around her. She had been to airports before, but this one was so completely foreign feeling that she worried she'd never find her way through it if separated from Jeremiah and Solomon.

Jeremiah must trust Solomon or they wouldn't be letting him lead the way. After what had happened on the plane she wasn't sure she was going to trust anyone she didn't know again.

So much had changed in the last day that it left her head spinning. She even knew Jeremiah's real name, something she'd been sure he'd never tell her. Malachi Abram was a very Biblical sounding name. She much preferred Jeremiah Silverman, though. Maybe that was just because it was the name she was familiar with.

She felt like she was being watched, but couldn't detect anyone following them or staring for any length of time. Maybe she was just being paranoid. She hoped that Solomon was worthy of Jeremiah's trust, and that he wasn't leading them into a trap.

Both men walked with long, purposeful strides and she practically had to jog to keep up with them. Until she had the lay of the land down better she didn't intend to let Jeremiah out of her sight for even a second.

They quickly collected Jeremiah and Cindy's luggage. Jeremiah started to head for the customs station, but Solomon touched his arm. "We have made alternate arrangements. We do not want it known that you are in the country if it can be helped."

Jeremiah glanced at Cindy.

"I assume she is in need of a Visa to enter?" Solomon asked.

Jeremiah nodded. Aaron had already provided Jeremiah with one, ostensibly courtesy of his former employers. That, too, was suspect now.

"We shall take care of that, too. Come."

They headed for a door in the far wall that had no markings on it but was still being watched over by two guards. Solomon flashed something to them and a moment later he, Jeremiah, and Cindy were through the door and heading down a staircase. Jeremiah noticed that the stairwell was filled with security cameras which all appeared to be turned off.

"You're taking a lot of precautions," he noted.

"There is a reason for it," Solomon said.

At the bottom they exited through another door that was heavily guarded. Steps away was a limousine with its windows blackened for privacy. The driver got out and opened the door for them. The three of them piled in and the driver returned to the front. Moments later they were in motion.

Solomon put up the privacy screen between them and the driver then he leaned back in his seat with a sigh. "I am sorry, my friend, that we meet again under such circumstances."

"Me, too. Care to tell me why?"

Solomon's eyes drifted to Cindy who had not said a word beyond the greeting she had given him. Her eyes were still wide with fear, but she was putting on a brave face. He needed to be able to keep her as close as possible no matter what was happening.

"Anything you have to say to me you can say in front of my wife," Jeremiah said, hoping that Cindy wouldn't flinch.

She didn't. Apparently they'd played that card often enough in hospitals and other sticky situations that she wasn't surprised.

Solomon, on the other hand, was.

"I had no idea you had gotten married," he said, doubt in his voice.

"We eloped a few days ago. We didn't want to deal with Cindy's family. We were planning on telling our friends at their party yesterday, but a more pressing matter came up," Jeremiah said, reaching out and taking Cindy's hand.

"You seem to be lacking wedding bands," Solomon observed.

"They're at the jeweler being resized. They didn't have the ones we liked available in our sizes on the way to the wedding. We were supposed to pick them up Tuesday," Cindy said.

Jeremiah was impressed with her quick thinking.

"Mazel tov. Hopefully when this is over I will be able to get you a wedding present."

"Going home would be enough of a present," Jeremiah said.

"No doubt. Your honeymoon has been inconveniently interrupted. I understand."

"Yes, and we'd like to know why. What was so important that you need my help? I've been out of things for a few years."

"Yes, but skills like yours are always in demand."

Jeremiah stiffened. He should have told Cindy everything about his time in the Mossad. Most pointedly, exactly what his job had been that required the skills Solomon was no doubt referring to.

"I was retired for a reason," Jeremiah reminded the other man.

"Yes, that was an unfortunate situation," Solomon said.

There were other adjectives Jeremiah would have chosen, but now was not the time to debate that.

"Actually, what we need most from you right now are your contacts."

"My contacts?" Jeremiah asked, puzzled. "Surely you know who most of them are."

"Yes, but things are very volatile right now. Very dangerous. Some people won't talk to us that we desperately need to share information with. You had a reputation for being trustworthy. You had contacts even among Arab intelligence operatives."

"They just found me amusing because I could quote the Koran better than most of them, particularly the verses where it stresses that Jews and Christians are not infidels but should be treated as weaker brothers."

"Whatever the reason, you have the ability to talk to some people that no one else can at this point and it is vital that we find a way to work together in the coming days."

"I know that the C.I.A. has increased its presence in the area. I also know that you're recalling agents other than me. All of this points to something really big about to happen."

"Unfortunately, we have reason to believe that what's about to happen will completely change everything and will plunge the entire region into war. That war will pull in other countries from outside the region until we are all trapped in World War III."

Jeremiah blinked. When he had known Solomon the man had not been prone to exaggerations. He looked deadly serious at the moment which led Jeremiah to believe that what he was saying was true, even if unthinkable.

"There are some on both sides who would welcome such a war, even at the threat of extinction."

Jeremiah frowned. "There's only one thing I can think of that would cause such a chain reaction. It would have to affect Kipat Hasela."

"Unfortunately, someone else has thought of that same thing, and that's what we've gotten wind of."

Solomon shifted his eyes again to Cindy. "My dear, you are familiar with the Temple, are you not?"

"The one built in Jerusalem by the Biblical Solomon? Yes," Cindy said.

"And what else do you know?"

"It was destroyed. Prophecy states that before the end of the world comes it will be rebuilt."

Solomon nodded approval. "And do you know why it has not already been rebuilt?"

Cindy nodded slowly. "I believe that on the location there is currently a Muslim mosque."

"That is correct. There is also a shrine, the Dome of the Rock, which is one of the most sacred sites for Muslims. Where it sits is holy ground for Muslims, Jews, and Christians. While it stands the Temple can not be rebuilt."

Cindy turned to stare at Jeremiah who nodded slowly.

"What are you saying?" Cindy asked, her voice little more than a whisper.

"Only this. Someone is planning to blow up the Dome of the Rock."

9

"I'm glad the baby's going to be born on the fifth," Mark said suddenly.

Geanie and Joseph, who had both had their heads bowed and their eyes closed, looked up at him, startled.

"It's not fair to a kid when they have to share their birthday with a holiday. A guy I went to school with was born on Christmas. He hated it. He didn't even get extra presents."

Geanie nodded slowly. She probably thought he was crazy for talking like this when everything hung in uncertainty. He couldn't stand the dark thoughts chasing each other through his mind anymore, though. He needed some happy thoughts, or, at least, non-depressing ones. Otherwise he was going to go crazy.

"I read somewhere once that one of the presidents had a daughter born on the Fourth of July and that she grew up thinking the fireworks were for her," Joseph chimed in.

"Can you imagine?" Mark said. "Here, Crystal, your dad's just a poor working stiff, but he's gotten people from all over to set off fireworks just for you." He was trying to make a joke, but he got a lump in his throat. "It's a girl, you know. Traci didn't want to know, but I did."

"Congratulations," Geanie said.

"I hope so. I hope everything is okay. I want to be able to see her, hold her, through the good times and the bad. I want to give her the best birthday parties she could ever have even though I won't ever be able to give her the pony she'll always ask for. Don't little girls always ask for ponies?"

"I did," Geanie answered.

"I wouldn't worry about the pony," Joseph said.

Mark took a ragged breath. "I know, I'm getting ahead of myself. Given what's happening I might not even have a little girl to raise."

"That's not what I meant," Joseph said quickly. "I meant that you don't have to worry about getting her a pony because her Aunt Geanie and her Uncle Joseph will get her one. And we'll get her the riding lessons to go along with it."

"You guys would do that?" Mark asked.

"In a heartbeat," Geanie said.

"Look, we don't plan on having children of our own for a few years, and neither of us have any siblings, any nieces or nephews to spoil silly, so we're going to have to play Aunt and Uncle to our friends' kids," Joseph said with a warm smile.

"I don't know if I should be grateful or afraid," Mark admitted.

"Be afraid. Very, very afraid," Geanie said with a wicked smile.

It actually made him smile for a moment. Then he shook his head. "Why is it that it seems like our little cadre is always in crisis mode?"

"Well, not always. After all, until a couple of hours ago none of us had stepped foot in a hospital for four months. That has to be some sort of record," Geanie said with a wan smile.

Mark shook his head. "I could go four lifetimes without ever being in a hospital again."

Cindy tried to take in everything that Solomon was saying. Jeremiah looked worried and even if she hadn't known anything about history, prophecy, religion, or politics his expression would have been enough to tell her that what they were dealing with was very, very bad. A few years back they'd had a guest pastor speak on Revelation and the end times. He had talked about the rebuilding of the Temple and it had made the whole thing seem far away since she knew that the site for the Temple was occupied by another structure at that point. Of course, she had never really stopped to think about the fact that one good sized explosion could change all of that.

"We don't know where the threat is coming from?" Jeremiah said.

"No. Everyone is accusing everyone. Naturally fingers are being pointed at us since who wants to see the Temple rebuilt more than Israelis? Of course, there are others who theorize that Muslim extremists are behind it."

That seemed strange to Cindy. Why would they want to blow up one of their sacred places? She kept her mouth shut, though. It was better to listen than speak in this situation.

Jeremiah was nodding slowly. "Because Jewish extremists would be the obvious ones to blame for such an act, it would give Arab nations a chance to strike at Israel with impunity."

"Yes, since most of the civilized world would object to the destruction of a holy place."

"But even if they believed Israel was responsible, her allies would not allow her to be destroyed completely."

"Hence, World War III. Of course, there is also the very real possibility that neither Arabs nor Jews are to blame for this coming disaster."

"Some countries would have a lot to gain from a war in this region."

"Precisely. There are intelligence operatives from dozens of countries crawling all over right now. All have heard the rumors. None can determine where they come from."

"Or if they're even true," Jeremiah countered.

Solomon nodded. "That had occurred to me as well. It could be a scare tactic, though to what end I'm not certain. It could also be an attempt to divert attention away from something else."

"From a real attack somewhere else entirely?" Jeremiah asked.

"Perhaps. Whatever it is, we have to find the truth."

"Did any of these rumors have any connection to Iran?" Jeremiah asked.

"Yes, how did you guess?"

Jeremiah shrugged, but didn't answer.

"A few months ago a boy was admitted to a hospital, very sick with a high fever. He'd been found wandering in the desert. While in the hospital he began to rave that the men who were going to destroy Qubbat As-Sakhrah had killed his brother. Both a C.I.A. agent being treated for a broken arm and one of our agents working locally undercover heard him."

"The boy could have been hallucinating."

"That seemed to be the consensus. That is, until the boy was found dead in his room, smothered by a pillow. That same night one of the young nurses on staff disappeared. For the last few months everyone's been scrambling, trying to get more information. Unfortunately, the boy's body disappeared and no one knew who he was or where he came from.

"Then, four days ago, the nurse showed up in Jerusalem, dead with his throat cut. There was one witness, a woman who was hidden from sight, who heard the nurse arguing with another man."

"What were they arguing about?"

"She wasn't sure, but it had something to do with the timing of an event. The killer kept insisting something would happen in two weeks. The victim argued that it was better to wait until Tish'a B'Av because of the symbolism. They started fighting and the victim ended up dead."

Jeremiah turned to look at Cindy. "Tish'a B'Av is a fast day that commemorates the destruction of the first two Temples. Making it a perfect symbolic day to destroy the one thing standing in the way of the Temple being rebuilt. It's just a few weeks away."

"But apparently, his co-conspirator didn't want to wait that long."

"And now we have a little over a week to stop him and those he's working with."

"Yes."

Cindy could feel her heart racing. That was barely any time, especially since it sounded like they were trying to find a needle in a haystack.

"So, where do I come in? You're wanting me to talk to some Arab contacts I used to have, is that right?"

"For the most part."

Cindy really didn't like the sound of that. That meant there was more that they wanted from him, and they just weren't willing to admit yet what that was. Odds were it was the worst part of the job. She expected Jeremiah to push for more information, but before he could she felt the limo swerve slightly to the right.

Moments later the limo came to a halt and Solomon nodded. "We will talk more tonight. I have a few things I must take care of now and the two of you need to get some rest, particularly after your most unpleasant flight."

Tired as she was Cindy felt like she might never sleep again. At least, not until these madmen were stopped. She managed to keep a sarcastic retort off her lips, but just barely.

Solomon pulled a keycard out of his pocket and handed it to Jeremiah. "Room 437. I trust you'll make yourself comfortable."

Jeremiah took the card from him just as the driver opened the door for them to get out. Jeremiah stepped out first with Cindy practically stepping on his heels. The driver retrieved their luggage from the trunk as she noticed that they were standing in front of what appeared to be a nice hotel.

Jeremiah took her hand and they entered the lobby, rolling their suitcases behind them. Without hesitation he made his way straight to the elevators. Less than a minute later they were entering their room.

It was larger than she would have expected with a sitting area to the right and the bedroom area with a king sized bed to the left. Seeing it drove home to Cindy just how tired and sleepy she really was. She glanced back at the sitting area. At least there was a couch. It didn't look as comfortable as the bed, but she should volunteer to take it since it was far more important that Jeremiah get good sleep than she did.

"I'll take-"

He turned and placed his hand over her mouth, cutting her off. She stared at him in surprise. He shook his head slowly and then very deliberately moved his hand and tugged on her ear.

He thought the place was bugged and that they were being listened to. She remembered how the C.I.A. agent had bugged her phone and hotel room in Las Vegas when she'd been visiting her brother in the hospital. She nodded her understanding. Next he pointed to his eyes and then to her.

She picked up instantly on what he was trying to say. Not only were they being listened to, they were being watched as well. She shivered, feeling intensely uncomfortable at the thought. It reminded her of how she had felt at the airport when she thought they were being watched. Only this was ten times worse because she knew it was true.

"I know it's been a long journey and you're exhausted," Jeremiah said, turning and moving farther into the room.

"I am. You must be, too."

"I am. Is it okay if I use the bathroom first?"

"Fine." She really needed to use the restroom but the thought that there might be cameras in there freaked her out.

Jeremiah rolled his suitcase to the closet, opened it, grabbed a few things, and headed for the bathroom. Three minutes later he emerged wearing only a pair of boxer shorts and a T-shirt. He walked over to her smiling.

"You look beautiful, neshama."

He put his arms around her and hugged her close, startling her. He put his lips against her ear and her skin tingled. "No camera in the bathroom," he whispered.

She nodded slightly, relieved at the information, but completely distracted by the embrace. He pulled away from her and smiled at her.

She managed to smile back. She put her suitcase in the closet, grabbed her pajamas and toiletry bag and headed into the bathroom. Jeremiah had packed her pajamas that had cavorting cats on them.

She changed clothes quickly and brushed her teeth. When she emerged a few minutes later she saw that Jeremiah had turned down the covers and was sitting on the edge of the bed. He stood up and walked back over to her. He hugged her again, but this time she was more prepared for it. When his lips touched her ear he whispered, "Trust me."

"Always," she whispered back.

He picked her up, twirled her around twice, and then set her down on the bed. Her heart was racing as she grabbed the covers and laid down, pulling them up to her chin. Jeremiah turned off the lights in the room, but there was still some light filtering through the curtains over the window.

He walked around to the other side of the bed and laid down, pulling the covers up as well. "Come here," he said, stretching out his arm.

Her heart in her throat she scooted closer to him. He wrapped his arm around her and pulled her close so that her head was resting on his chest. "I'll take care of you," he said.

"I know you will," she answered.

"I know this is not the honeymoon you were hoping for. I'm sorry."

"All I need is to be with you," she said, heart pounding out of control.

He opened his eyes and looked at her. "That's very distracting. Come on, we're supposed to be getting some sleep. We're both exhausted."

She wasn't sure if he was referring to her pounding heart or if this was just the next line in the little drama they were putting on for whoever might be watching and listening.

"I can't help it. You know I get excited whenever I'm this close to you," she said.

He squeezed her shoulder. "Goodnight."

"Goodnight."

She closed her eyes and tried to calm herself down so she could fall asleep.

"Ani ohev otach," he said softly after a minute.

She didn't answer because she didn't know what he had said.

Jeremiah was awake long after Cindy had fallen asleep. He'd had the best intentions of going to sleep, but it was hard to do so when so many thoughts and feelings were crashing through him.

Ani ohev otach. He had told her he loved her. He hadn't meant to, it had just slipped out. To anyone listening it would have sounded completely natural because it was. He did love her and drowsing there with her head on his shoulder it was impossible not to think about it.

There were a dozen other things he should be thinking about, but she was the only one that his thoughts would linger on. Every time he tried to think of something different his mind returned moments later to her.

He owed her his life.

He also owed her the truth. About everything.

She had handled herself really well all day and he could not have been more proud. It was funny, the marriage lie was becoming easier and easier to tell. One of these days even he was going to start believing it. Then again, that was wishful thinking.

Cindy moaned softly in her sleep and he wondered if she was having a nightmare. He'd give everything he had to keep nightmares from her waking moments as well as her sleeping ones. Somehow that didn't seem meant to be, though. All he could do was be there to hold her hand as she walked through them.

He took several slow, cleansing breaths. The night would come soon enough and he had to be ready when it did.

Mark was dreaming that he and Traci were back on the beach in Tahiti, soaking up the sun and laughing like they didn't have a care in the world. He kept glancing at the horizon, though, and he could see dark storm clouds in the distance. He told himself that there was no need to worry because they were so far away. So he kissed Traci's nose and that made her smile. Then he looked again and the clouds were closer, much closer. How had they moved so fast? He frowned, not wanting them to spoil their time together.

Traci didn't seem to care. She didn't see the clouds, but he did. They were large and thick and ominous and the winds of change were blowing them hard and fast until they were advancing at a terrifying pace.

The rain's coming, he told Traci.

She just laughed and kissed him.

She didn't understand. She didn't know what he knew. The clouds were coming for them and would be there before they knew it. They needed to seek shelter while they could.

Don't leave me, Traci said as he started to get up.

How could he make her understand if she didn't see the storm coming? The waves began to creep higher and higher up the sand, reaching out for them with foamy hands as though seeking to pull them out to sea where they would be lost forever.

Traci, get up, we have to run! She just smiled at him. Before he could say anything else something touched his shoulder, shaking him.

"Mark, wake up."

He came to and realized that he had drifted off in the waiting room. Geanie was gently shaking his shoulder.

"What is it?" he asked groggily.

"Someone's coming," she said, voice tense.

He heard footsteps and rose out of the chair. The dream faded into the background, but the fear he had felt during it was only magnified now that he was awake.

A doctor walked in. He was haggard, had dark circles under his eyes and looked like he needed sleep just as badly as Mark did.

"Do you have news?" Mark asked, voice terse.

The doctor nodded. "You might want to sit down."

10

Mark swayed on his feet. "Traci, is she okay?"

"She's going to be fine," the doctor told him.

Relief flooded him. His wife was going to be okay. A moment later, though, his stomach clenched again. If she was fine then what had gone wrong?

"And the baby?" Mark asked, barely able to get the words out.

"That's the shocking part. I'm not sure how this happened, but every once in a while we'll get a surprise like this."

"A surprise? What surprise?"

"Congratulations, Detective Walters, you are the father of twins."

"Twins?" Mark asked, not sure he had heard right.

"Yes. A boy and a girl. They both appear to be healthy and they are just beautiful."

Geanie and Joseph were patting him on the back congratulating him. He felt like he was still dreaming. "When can I see them?"

"The nurses are cleaning up the babies and you can see them in a little while. You can see your wife now although she's still pretty groggy. Um, just you for now. When she's a little more with it the others can come in."

"We'll be here waiting," Joseph said.

Mark nodded and followed the doctor from the room. Twins. It was unbelievable. His mind was reeling from the implications. He had a son as well as a daughter. They were going to have to get more baby furniture. In a couple of years they were probably going to have to get a bigger house.

When he walked into the hospital room and saw Traci laying in the bed, pale, but awake and smiling at him all the pain and fear of the last several hours evaporated. He rushed to her side and kissed her.

"Are you okay?" he asked when he finally pulled away.

"Better now."

"It's a good thing we painted the nursery green," he said with a sudden laugh.

"It is," she said, her smile broadening.

He pulled up the chair and sat down on it. Then he reached forward and took her hand. "You really had me scared there for a while."

"Sorry. A nurse told me that sometimes twins come early. I guess they got tired of sharing a room."

"Well, they're going to have to share one at the house, at least for a little while," he said.

She nodded.

"And don't worry. I'll do everything I can while you're recovering to make this easy on you."

She raised an eyebrow.

"Okay, easier."

She raised the other eyebrow.

"Okay, not as nightmarish as it could possibly be."

"That sounds about right." Her smile faded. "I'm sorry you weren't there to see it."

"It's okay. As tired and scared as I was, maybe I would have just passed out and embarrassed you."

"I have a hard time picturing the veteran police detective passing out at the sight of a little blood."

"It could happen. Wouldn't be the first time something like that did, I'm sure," he said.

"I'm glad you're okay with it."

"You're healthy, the babies are healthy. We have more than one baby. What more could a man ask for?"

"Well, I don't know about a man, but a woman would like to settle on names so we can call them by their names."

"Okay. I know you're leaning toward Rachel for a girl's name."

"And you prefer Crystal."

"How about this? We name our daughter Rachel and our son Ryan?"

Traci nodded. "Ryan, I like it."

"Then it's settled. We can tell them what to put on the birth certificates."

"Ah, but what about middle names?"

"This is going to sound crazy, but I was kind of thinking Rachel Jean and Ryan Joe."

Traci smiled. "Variants on Geanie and Joseph's names?"

"Well, they have been in the waiting room with me all night. And we know that Jeremiah wouldn't approve of us using his name as long as he's alive, so there you go."

"I like it."

"Then it's settled."

"Do you think they're okay? Cindy and Jeremiah?"

"I hope so," Mark said fervently. "I just wish there was something I could do to help them."

"You were saying that you thought one of your older cases could be linked."

"It's possible. It's also possible that I'm crazy."

"Well, that's more than possible, it's probable. I don't know, though, I keep getting this strong feeling that you should keep digging. Who knows, maybe you will find something that will help them?"

Mark nodded. "I will, but tomorrow. Right now all I'm interested in doing is being with my beautiful wife and our amazing kids."

"Look who we have here," a female voice said behind him.

Mark turned and watched as two nurses walked in, each carrying an infant in their arms. "Your daughter," the first nurse said, handing Mark the tiniest baby he had ever seen.

"Your son," the second nurse said, carefully lowering the second baby into Traci's arms.

"They're so small. Are you sure they're going to be okay?" Mark asked.

"The doctor was checking them over. So far, so good, although we'll be keeping them here for a little while just to make sure. Plus, there are still several important things to do like see if they can feed."

"Well, what are we waiting for?" Traci asked.

"And afterwards we need to introduce them to the Aunt and Uncle who are getting them ponies," Mark said.

Jeremiah was scared. He hadn't felt this way in a long, long time. Everything that was going on, the disaster that he had been called in to help avert, having Cindy here in the line of fire were all making him sweat. He was terrified of losing her. But he was almost more terrified of her finally seeing him for who he really was and realizing she wanted no part of him.

She was asleep on his shoulder and he wished they could stay like that forever. He liked looking out for her, protecting her. He kept having the terrible, sinking feeling that this would be the last few moments they ever spent at peace with life and each other.

There was a high probability that one or both of them would get killed. There was an even higher probability that they would be forever changed or scarred by what was to come. He wanted to savor this moment, make it last forever.

Because as soon as they woke up and faced the day everything was going to change. She would look at him differently. She would see the monster inside. These few moments before that happened were a sanctuary, stolen treasures for him to lock up in his heart and ponder for the rest of his life, however long that might be.

Even now he could feel her waking, though. Her breathing was shifting. Any moment now and he'd lose her. He ached inside, already feeling the loss. It was as though he was a drowning man, clutching at straws hoping that he could still be saved. He only wished he could be.

Cindy woke with a start. She jerked hard and twisted her head to see Jeremiah staring intently at her.

"Good afternoon," he said without smiling.

"Afternoon."

She had her head on his shoulder and an arm flung over his chest. Flushing she started to sit up, but he pulled her

109

back down. He ran his hand slowly up and down her arm. Her skin felt hot and cold where he was touching it.

"Things are going to get a lot worse from here," he said.

"I know."

"I can't let the destruction of the shrine occur. I can't have the world plunged into war."

"Of course not. That would be unthinkable."

"Everyone is going to have to do their best, be their best in order to stop this."

"I understand," she said, still distracted by his hand stroking her arm.

"I'm not sure you do."

He ran his hand down to hers then laced his fingers through hers.

"I'm going to have to be the man I used to be. I never wanted to have to be that man. And I never, ever wanted you to have to see that man."

"Jer...Malachi, it's okay," she said, his real name unfamiliar on her tongue.

He closed his eyes with a little groan. "I know this is going to sound strange but I both love and hate hearing you say my name like that."

She didn't know what to say. She was pretty sure the conversation they were having wasn't for the benefit of any listeners, but she could also tell that he didn't care if they were listening. She was just glad she hadn't slipped completely and called him Jeremiah.

"Malachi," she said softly although she wasn't sure what drove her to say it.

He let go of her hand and wrapped both arms around her, crushing her tight to him. He buried his face in her neck and his breath tickled.

"I don't want you to see the monster I have been," he whispered.

Her heart was hammering in her chest and her entire body felt warm and tingly. She put her hand on his head and began to stroke his hair.

"I know what you are, and all I see is a man."

His lips pressed against her neck and she gasped at the sensation.

"Cindy, my darling, my love, you bring out the best in me. But right now I need to tap into the worst of me."

He kissed her neck again, his arms tightening even more around her. His breathing sounded ragged. "I need you to go home," he whispered in between more kisses to her neck. His lips trailed up to her ear and he kissed it as well. "I need you to be safe."

He rolled slightly and pulled her on top of him as he continued to kiss and nuzzle her neck. "I need you to be there. I need you to wait for me. Because if I make it out of this alive, I'm going to need you to remind me how to be a good man again."

"I don't need to remind you; you know on your own," she said, gasping slightly for air. Her thoughts were scattering. She could feel him underneath her. She could feel his fear, his need. She felt the hunger in his lips as they trailed across her throat.

"Cindy, I'm already slipping away, I can feel it," he said, looking up at her. His eyes were pleading. "I need you to go home to Pine Springs. I need to hold on to the hope that someday I can go back there again. And maybe you can remind me what it was like to be a rabbi, a friend, all those things that I am there that I'm not here."

"I'm not leaving you."

She dipped her head and kissed his cheek. She felt dizzy, breathless.

He buried his head in her neck again. "I don't deserve your kiss. You don't know the things I've done."

"I don't care what you've done. That's in the past. This is about the present."

He started shaking, his body shuddering hard and she could feel his tears against her skin.

"I'm so sorry," he kept saying over and over.

"For what?"

He grew very still. Slowly he sat up. He twisted her so that she was sitting on the edge of the bed. He let go of her and stood up. His eyes were closed as he turned to face her.

"I'm sorry that you're going to have to see everything I've tried to hide from you," he said.

His voice was different. His accent was thicker, but it was more than that. There was a hardness to it that she'd only ever noticed a few times before. He drew a deep breath and then he opened his eyes.

Where she usually saw warmth and humor and compassion now she only saw cold, calculating rage.

11

Cindy stared up at Jeremiah, and it was almost like seeing a stranger staring back. She steeled herself for whatever was going to come next.

"I will ask you once more and it will be the last. Will you leave this place and go to safety?" he asked.

She stood slowly and clenched her hands into fists at her side. "No. I will stand by you. Whatever the cost."

He nodded. "Let's get dressed. They'll be coming for us soon." He turned and went to the closet. He reached into her suitcase and pulled out some clothes then walked back over and placed them on the bed. "Wear these."

He had chosen a long black skirt that reached to her ankles and a long sleeved black blouse that he must have dug out of the back of her closet since she barely could remember it. She was pretty sure it was too big on her and that was why it had been relegated to the back of the closet, awaiting the day she would finally clean out the unwanted clothes and donate them to charity.

Sitting on top of the blouse was a black scarf her mother had given her for Christmas a couple of years before. It had been typical of her mom to give her something she would never use.

"What do I do with this?" Cindy asked, picking up the scarf.

"Cover your head with it. Tuck your hair inside so it doesn't show. I can help you wrap it if you need me to."

Cindy stared for a moment at the scarf. If she made it back to California she might have to call her mother and thank her.

Jeremiah pulled off his T-shirt and Cindy couldn't help but stare at his chest for a moment. Every muscle in his torso was well-defined. The clothes he wore just never showed it off.

What her eyes gravitated to most, though, were the scars. There were so many of them. She knew he'd gotten one of them in the army during hand-to-hand combat training. The rest had to have come from his time working with the Mossad.

He turned toward the closet and she saw that his back had its fair share of scars as well. He grabbed some clothes out of his suitcase and turned around. He caught her staring, but she didn't avert her eyes.

"At least now you know where the scars come from," he said.

"In the general sense, yes. I still don't know how you actually got each one."

"They're not pretty stories."

"I wouldn't expect them to be. Not if they leave those kinds of scars," she said. *And the psychological ones are pretty brutal as well*, she thought to herself.

She crossed to the closet, grabbed some underwear from her bag, then picked up the clothes on the bed and headed into the bathroom. Ten minutes later she was dressed and ready with the exception of the scarf which was giving her trouble. She didn't have any hair pins or scrunchies to help her put her hair up and it kept escaping from the scarf.

Mindful of the fact that people could be listening she opened the door. "Malachi, I'm going to need help with the scarf after all."

"Shortly," he called.

She exited the bathroom, scarf in hand.

"It just won't stay..." she stumbled to a halt. Solomon and Jeremiah were sitting in two of the chairs in the living area of the room. Solomon must have arrived just after she went into the bathroom since Jeremiah still had his shirt off.

"I'm sorry," she said.

"I am the one who is intruding," Solomon said.

"What's wrong with the scarf?" Jeremiah asked.

"It keeps slipping on my head and I can't get my hair to stay up since I don't have any pins. Does the hotel have a sundries store that might carry something?" she asked, keeping one eye warily on Solomon.

"I don't expect so. That's okay. I have a simple solution."

Jeremiah got up and headed to the closet. He pulled something out of his bag. "Okay, turn around," he instructed.

She did so, holding the scarf in one hand and pulling back her hair with the other. He came up behind her and lifted the hair off her neck. A moment later something cold touched her neck and then she heard a terrible ripping sound.

"Done," Jeremiah said.

She turned and saw that he was holding several inches of her hair in one hand and a long, sharp knife in another.

She gasped and her hand flew up to feel her head. He had cut off so much of her hair that what was left didn't even reach to the collar of her shirt.

"How dare you?" she fumed, shocked that he had done it at all let alone without her permission.

"He was right to do so. Where you are going it would be very dangerous for you to have your hair exposed. This will make it easier on you," Solomon said.

Jeremiah walked into the bathroom and came back after having dumped her hair in the garbage. He took her scarf and began to wrap it around her head.

"And where is it we're going?" she asked, still angry.

"Iran," he said.

Iran. The very thought of going there made her suddenly queasy and her anger was quickly replaced by fear.

"I don't want to go there," she whispered.

"No, you don't. I would recommend you stay here and wait for him," Solomon said.

"She's not staying behind," Jeremiah said grimly. Finished wrapping her head he stepped back. He nodded shortly as though to signal that he was pleased with the work then turned and walked back toward Solomon. "We have less than two weeks so we'll need to move fast," Jeremiah said.

"I'd prefer to do this another way, but we just don't have the time. You'll be flying in by way of Frankfurt. You have first class tickets."

"Cover?"

"Rich German businessman and his American wife looking to invest locally. You'll be staying at the Evin Parsian Hotel."

"I don't like going in so high profile."

"I don't like it either, but it's fast and that's what we need. I'll be sending a man with you posing as your assistant."

"No."

"What do you mean?"

"No one goes with us. It's just Cindy and me."

"But the man I'm sending is one of the best."

"I don't care. The last man you sent was killed and I very nearly was, too. Any ideas yet on who the imposter was or who sent him after me?"

Solomon grimaced. "He was one of ours. Missing, presumed dead, six months ago."

"That's exactly why it's just going to be the two of us. Did you handle the arrangements yourself?"

"I did."

"Good."

Cindy felt lost as she listened to the two men discussing the impending trip to Iran. Everything in her screamed that this was a bad idea. What choice did she have, though? She wasn't leaving Jeremiah, so if he was going to Iran then so was she.

"I don't have any clothes that look like what the wife of a rich European would wear," Cindy protested. She touched her hand to the scarf around her head. "I don't exactly have the glamorous hairstyle either."

"The clothes we have for you. Short hair is in style," Solomon said, a look of irritation crossing his face before he turned back to Jeremiah.

Cindy's fear began to give way to a second wave of anger. Jeremiah's cutting of her hair had been unnecessary as it turned out.

"Once you're on the ground in Tehran what will you need from us?"

"Nothing. I will handle it. I will need you to ease any agents you already have there back and away from us without telling them why. The last thing I need is to have to worry about bumping into one of them."

"I'll do what I can."

"There is one other thing I'll need."

"What's that?"

"Exit plans. Several of them, because I'm certain there's no way we'll be leaving the country the same way we got there."

Cindy felt a chill dance up her spine. That sounded ominous and she found the fear creeping back. After all, what did it matter what length her hair was if she was dead?

It was late when Traci finally sent Mark home to get some rest. As much as he didn't want to leave, he knew she was right. He was running on fumes and pretty soon he was going to collapse if he didn't get at least a couple hours sleep. Geanie and Joseph had left several hours earlier after getting to visit with Traci and see the babies.

Babies.

He was still trying to wrap his head around the fact that he had twins. It was wonderful and terrifying all at the same time.

He got home and half-staggered to the front door. He made it inside and turned on the lights. The house was silent. He took a deep breath as he realized that it was just the calm before a very long storm.

118

Out of habit he reached for Buster's leash, but it wasn't hanging on the hook. He blinked in surprise for a moment until he remembered that he had given Geanie and Joseph a key so that they could come and get Buster and Captain and take them to their house for a few days. Both dogs had likely been thrilled when they showed up to give them their morning walk. It freed him up not to have to worry about them getting outside to use the bathroom the next couple of days while he would be spending so much time at the hospital.

He'd also called Liam from the hospital, and, after sharing the good news, asked him to find out as much as he could about the Iranian student's family. Hopefully he'd come up with something soon that would be of help.

Mark headed back to the bedroom and barely managed to get undressed before he fell into bed. The moment his head hit the pillow he was asleep.

Jeremiah had to admit that Cindy looked exceptional in a designer dress. She'd even managed to fluff out her now short hair into an appealing look. He knew she was angry about that, but she'd be using the scarf soon enough and she'd be grateful for the short hair then.

The flight to Frankfurt had been fine although spent mostly in silence. That had been good, though, as it had given him time to plan and think. There were three men he could possibly talk to in the country. Fortunately Solomon had had an easy time locating the whereabouts of one of them. His daughter was about to get married in an elaborate ceremony which would make it easier to approach him publically than it normally would have.

Finding the other two would be far more challenging. One of them he couldn't even get confirmation whether or not the man was still alive. There'd be a lot of scrambling to do once they hit the ground.

They'd left their own clothes and suitcases back in the hotel in Tel Aviv. They were traveling with just one suitcase now with a mixture of clothing styles for both of them. Jeremiah had had to leave the knife he cut Cindy's hair with behind as well. He did have on him a small, black knife made out of incredibly tough plastic. It had gone with him everywhere he went when he was working for the Mossad. The small knife didn't show up on metal detectors, but was sharp enough and strong enough to make killing someone easy.

Their flight to Tehran was going to be boarding in half an hour and Cindy had gone to use the restroom. He stood up casually and walked toward the restrooms, searching out all the cameras in the place.

There were none focused on the water fountains near the women's room. Jeremiah took a drink then lingered there waiting for Cindy. A moment later she emerged and was clearly startled to see him right there.

"Come here," he said.

She took the few steps to him and then stopped right next to him. "There's one more thing Solomon picked up for me before we left," he said, reaching into his pocket. He pulled out a ring box and opened it. Inside it was a platinum wedding band with diamonds on it.

"It's beautiful," she gasped.

"The wife of a wealthy businessman needs to display her jewels proudly," he said as he picked up her hand and slipped it on her finger.

From his pocket he retrieved a matching platinum man's wedding band and he slipped it on his hand. "There, now we look official," he said.

She nodded, unable to take her eyes off the ring on her finger. He let her stare at it for a moment more then he took her other hand and tugged slightly. "Let's get back to the gate."

"Okay," she said, her voice sounding somewhat strangled.

He understood. He was having problems not thinking about the weight of the ring on his own finger and everything that it symbolized. He was tired of living a lie, though. He wished it was all real.

But he couldn't afford to daydream like that. Not when there was work to be done.

When Mark woke up it was early morning. Sunlight was just starting to creep into the room. For a moment he drowsed, wondering what had woken him. Then he heard the chime on his phone that let him know he had a voice message. He twisted onto his side and grabbed the phone from the table next to the bed.

Maybe Traci was calling with a list of things he had to do to get ready to bring home two babies instead of one. He'd already started working on that list in his head the day before but had since forgotten half of it he was sure. No matter how well prepared he was he knew that once the Rachel and Ryan came home everything could change as the reality of what babies needed trumped their perceptions of what babies needed.

It turned out the message was from Liam. Mark pressed his ear to the phone to listen.

"You asked me to track down information on Asim Kazmi's family. It turns out he's got an uncle in Detroit. His parents are both dead, but he has two older brothers. One of them is still in Iran. The other moved to Jerusalem six months ago."

12

Mark's heart was pounding as he called Liam back.

"Hi, Mark, how's Traci?" Liam asked when he answered the phone.

"Doing well, so are Rachel and Ryan."

"I'm so glad to hear it. I'm planning on stopping by around lunchtime to see everyone."

"That would be wonderful. I know Traci would appreciate it," Mark said, battling his own impatience. "Look, I got your message. Have you talked to either of the brothers or the uncle yet?"

"No. I don't have numbers for the brothers, but I do have one for the uncle."

"I'm going to call him. Can you text it to me?"

"Sure, right away. Everything okay?"

"Yeah, why?"

"Given that Traci just had the babies and this is a day off for you, I would think this would be the last thing you'd be thinking about today."

"Yeah, well, I might have had a breakthrough. I want to follow up while the thoughts are fresh in mind. Maybe it's nothing."

Mark said goodbye and ended the call. Moments later the text from Liam came in and he stared at the number for a moment. Maybe it was nothing.

"Or maybe this will help save my friends' lives," he whispered.

He called the number then waited impatiently as it rang. Just when he thought it was going to go to voicemail a man answered. "Hello?"

"Hi, I'm looking for Mr. Kazmi."

"This is him."

"Sir, my name is Mark Walters, I'm one of the detectives who has been working to find your nephew's killer."

There was a pause and then the man spoke, his voice choked with emotion. "You cannot be working too hard at it since it has been two years and there has been no justice for Asim."

Mark closed his eyes and took a deep breath. Loved ones always thought that no matter how much effort police were putting in that it was never enough. Asim's uncle had more cause to complain than most. He needed the man on his side, though.

"One of the original detectives assigned to the case was murdered. I recently was able to look at the file and read over some of his notes that he hadn't entered into the official report. It's possible I've found something, but I need to ask you some questions to know if I'm even on the right track."

It was unfair of him, putting the blame on Paul that way. But Paul was dead and had left him with a heck of a mess, even if technically Asim's murder wasn't part of it. Besides, if the man he was talking to felt like he cared, like he was a new detective on the case doing his best, he would likely be less jaded and more cooperative.

"I am sorry to hear that."

"I appreciate that sir. He was a good man, but he left a mess behind him. It was only by sheer chance that I came across the one note that I did that got me thinking in a new light about the case."

"Perhaps it was not chance, but Allah guiding you in that discovery."

Mark hesitated a moment and then said, "For most of my life I haven't believed in God. The last couple of years, though, I've seen things that I couldn't explain any other way. Well, lately it's got me thinking quite a lot. You could be right."

"I know I'm right," the man said, his voice warming. "Now, tell me what I can do to help you find my nephew's killer."

"I appreciate it. First, I should ask you if this is a good time. I have a lot of questions. Some of them will seem quite basic or even unnecessary, but are important for me to see the entire picture."

"I understand, Detective, and for the man who will find Asim's killer I have all the time in the world."

"I appreciate that, sir. As I understand it, Asim's parents are both deceased. Is that correct?"

"Yes, it was a tragedy. They died when Asim was sixteen."

"What happened to them, if you don't mind my asking."

"A car accident. It was what you would call ironic."

"How so?"

"They were visiting some of my sister-in-law's family in Gaza. They had gone out for the evening by themselves and when they returned her family's home had been destroyed along with several of their neighbors. She lost six relatives that day."

"But she and her husband escaped the bombing?"

"Yes, only to be killed the next morning by a drunk driver. Senseless waste of life."

"Their sons weren't with them at the time?" Mark asked. He was definitely getting an image of how that tragedy could have affected their children.

"The oldest boy was with them. He survived the car accident, but was never the same. It scarred him physically, but more than that it twisted him and made him bitter, crazy. The second oldest boy was away at university. Asim was still in high school and stayed at home with friends. He had wanted to go with them, but his father refused to allow him to miss that many days of school. I told him Allah had persuaded his father to leave him behind so that he might live, grow to manhood and do something important with his life. I believed that with all my heart. But then some coward took that from him."

Mark struggled to find the words to say to make it better, but none came. All he could do was press on and try to find peace for this man and justice for his nephew as quickly as he could. "The boys lived all their lives in Iran, is that correct?" Mark asked, forcing the words out.

"Until that time, yes. I brought Asim here to live with me. He finished high school with honors. He got accepted to a wonderful college in California where he could study under some of the best minds in his field and I was happy to pay the tuition. I knew that he was going to do great things with his life, that he had been spared for a reason."

"His older brothers stayed in Iran?"

"Yes, Khalid returned there after he left the hospital. Tamir stayed in the university."

"You said that the accident changed Khalid?"

"Yes. His name means 'immortal'. He started to believe that it was true, that he didn't die with his parents because he could not die. His rage over what had happened grew deeper every day and the wounds that time should have healed instead became more raw with each passing day. He was sick, he had a disease of the mind, but I could not reason with him. After a while I stopped trying. Tamir was also bitter, but not in the same way. When he graduated from the university I offered to get him a job here where he could live a better life. He refused. He said he had no interest in the things of the West."

The man was painting a chilling picture, one that Mark didn't like at all. The more he heard, though, the more he believed that he had been right to be suspicious.

"I believe I have this in my notes, but could you tell me what Asim was studying here in California?"

"Certainly. He had a dual major and was going for degrees in both Sociology and Political Science. He had a dream of bringing peace to his homeland someday. He was so kind and gentle and well-spoken that some days I allowed myself to dream that he actually had a chance at doing that."

"From what I understand he was well-liked by his professors and peers."

"Yes. He had made many friends and I was happy for him. He even had a girlfriend, Amy, that he spoke almost constantly of when we'd talk on the phone."

"When was the last time you spoke to him?"

"The night before he died. We spoke at least once a week."

"How did he seem to you that night?"

"He was agitated. Upset. I pressed and he told me it was nothing. I persisted and he admitted to me that he had a fight with Amy, but that he was going to make everything alright."

"Did he say what they fought about?"

"No."

"Did he say anything else peculiar?"

"Yes, he did. He told me he'd make things right with her just as soon as he'd figured out who he needed to talk to about something important."

"Did he mention what that important thing might be?"

"No, I asked, but he wouldn't say, which was very unlike him. Asim never was the type to have secrets. It was the first time he'd ever kept something from me. He was always such a good boy, though. I knew that when he was ready he would tell me."

"Did he talk often with his brothers or other family members besides you?"

"Generally, not often. However, he did spend a week in Iran with his brothers about a month before he died."

"Why did he go back?"

"Tamir was getting married and Asim went for the celebration."

"Did you go?"

"No. I was not invited," the other man said, a trace of anger coloring his voice.

"Can you tell me anything more about his girlfriend, Amy? I don't remember seeing her name in the file."

"Her name was Amy Smith. I remember the first time he told me. He commented that it was a genuine American name and that seemed to please him for some reason."

"Did she go to college with him?"

"Yes, but she was in entirely different classes. He met her because she worked at the Starbucks by his house. He told me when he first saw her he went every day for a week before getting up the courage to ask her out."

"Do you happen to know what she looked like?"

"He sent me a picture, but I do not know if I still have it. She was a very pretty girl with red hair."

Mark was definitely going to have to look up Amy Smith. He knew for a fact her name hadn't come up in the original investigation and he couldn't help but wonder why.

"Mr. Kazmi, I want to thank you so much for your time," Mark said.

"Certainly. Please, call if there is anything else you need. And, I would appreciate it if you would call and let me know when you have found something."

"I will," Mark promised.

"Are there no other questions I can answer for you right now?"

Mark took a deep breath. "There is one, and I don't mean to cause offense."

"None will be taken."

"Is it possible that one or more of Asim's older brothers was or could be involved with something dangerous?"

There was a pause and Mark was sure that he had gone too far. When the man spoke again his voice was heavy with sorrow. "I understand what it is you are asking, Detective. For Tamir, I cannot say. I do not know him well enough."

"And Khalid?"

"Khalid was a hateful, twisted young man a few years ago. I have no doubt that without some extraordinary intervention by Allah that he has become an evil man capable of doing unspeakable things."

Mark licked his lips which suddenly felt very dry. "Thank you for your candor," he said.

"As I said at the beginning of the conversation, I will do anything I can to help the man that will bring Asim's murderer to justice."

"No matter where the trail may lead?" Mark asked before he could stop himself.

"I am not a violent man, but if I knew that Khalid was responsible I would take his life from him myself."

"Thank you, Mr. Kazmi. That's all I needed to know."

When Mark ended the call he realized that he was sweating heavily. A picture had formed in his head and he didn't like it one bit. He thought about calling Jeremiah, but he decided that he needed to double check one thing first.

He glanced at the clock. It was almost nine in the morning. It was time to get dressed and go see Traci, but first he figured he'd stop and get some coffee on the way.

Half an hour later Mark was walking into the Starbuck's that was closest to where Asim's apartment had been. It had been two years and the odds were against him finding Amy there. For all he knew she could have already graduated and moved halfway across the country. Before he started doing a people search for an Amy Smith, though, he figured it didn't hurt to check the place out.

The line was long. He was not going to wait that long for coffee, not with Traci waiting for him at the hospital. He walked around it and walked down the counter, looking at the people behind it. Two guys and a girl with dark hair. He was about to leave when a young woman who worked there exited the bathroom. She had flaming red hair that fell halfway down her back.

He moved to intercept her before she got behind the counter. "Amy Smith?" he asked.

She blinked at him in surprise. "Yes, who are you?"

He pulled out his badge. "Detective Mark Walters. I'd like to talk to you about Asim Kazmi."

She turned pale and for a moment he thought she might faint or run. After a moment she seemed to steady herself. "Give me a minute." She walked behind the counter and pulled aside one of the other baristas. She said something to him and then came back around the counter and led Mark outside.

She kept walking until they came to a shady spot under a tree far away from most of the cars clustered around the building. She stopped in the shade and turned to look at him. She wiped at her eyes which were tearing up.

"After he...he died, I thought for sure someone would come around to talk to me, but no one ever did."

"Why didn't you contact the police?"

She wrapped her arms around herself. "And say what? That my boyfriend and I had had a huge fight the day before he was killed? That would have made me look guilty."

"Hiding makes you look even more guilty," Mark advised gruffly.

"I couldn't cope. I know that's wrong and everything, but...I loved him, you know?"

"Prove it."

"How?" she asked, wiping more tears away.

"By helping me catch whoever killed him."

"I don't know who killed him," she protested.

"No, but you know something."

"I don't know. It was a long time ago, it seems like someone else's life sometimes, you know?"

"Two years is a long time to carry around guilt and grief. Don't you think you've suffered long enough?" he asked, changing tactics.

She began crying in earnest. "I was afraid...I don't even remember why now. Maybe I was afraid I'd get killed, too."

"By who?" Mark pressed, but kept his voice soft.

"I'm not sure. It was just weird you know. Everything was weird after he got back from his brother's wedding."

"How was it weird?"

"He was mad at them, but he wouldn't tell me about what. He kept saying that they were stupid and part of the problem instead of part of the solution. He said that their hate was poisoning them, but that they refused to see a different way."

"Go on."

"One of them called him about a week before he died, I don't know which one. He did tell me, though, that he realized he couldn't have anything more to do with them, maybe not ever."

"Did they call again?"

"No, but a few days later I saw him in the park talking to this...skank."

"A girl?"

"Yeah, tight black pants, plunging shirt. She was a real piece of work and she was coming on to him, trying to talk him into...heaven only knows what."

"I got mad and later that day I confronted him. He said she was noone. I said it looked like they were having a pretty long conversation for her to be noone. He said it was his problem and he actually told me to mind my own business. I was furious. I thought he was cheating on me. The next day I had cooled off and I realized Asim wasn't the kind of guy to ever cheat. I felt so bad. I was going to make him dinner and apologize, but...he was already dead."

"Do you think the woman had something to do with it?"

"I don't know, but whatever she said to him, it really upset him. I've never seen him like that."

Mark's heart went out to her. He encountered a lot of liars in his profession, but this girl was not one of them. "Don't be so hard on yourself. There's nothing you could have done to save him," he said.

"Maybe if I hadn't fought with him," she said, now crying openly.

"No, it wouldn't have mattered. And it's even possible that by distancing yourself for those few hours you saved your own life. His blood is not on your hands, and it's time to forgive yourself and let it go."

She was crying even harder now, great gasping sobs of pain, but after a minute he could tell that she was also experiencing some sense of release. That was good. She didn't need to be carrying this guilt around with her for the rest of her life. There'd eventually be plenty of things in life for her to be legitimately guilty over without making extra trouble for herself.

"Thank you," she said at last when her tears had subsided.

He handed her his card. "If you think of anything else, please let me know."

"I will," she promised.

He thought of Traci. He needed to go to her. He turned and started to walk away, but then turned back as one last thought occurred to him.

"The woman, was she Iranian?" Mark asked.

Amy shook her head. "No, she was Russian."

13

Cindy was a bundle of nerves by the time they arrived at the hotel in Iran. She kept fidgeting with the ring on her finger even though she knew she shouldn't. It just felt so foreign, like everything else around her. She had been surprised to discover on the plane that Jeremiah actually spoke German and with an accent good enough to fool the flight attendants. When she'd asked him how many other languages he spoke he just smiled at her.

"What do we do next?" she asked as she sat down on the edge of the bed.

"Next, we rest up for a few minutes. I'm going out tonight to try and find someone, and I really can't take you along to that meeting. Trust me, please on this. The best thing you can do is rest. Tomorrow afternoon we'll be heading out for a wedding where we'll be meeting a contact. Hopefully the man can help shed some light on this whole thing."

"Okay."

"The man we are going to see. His name is Omar. He loves proverbs."

"He's a friend of yours?"

"He would say so."

"And what do you say?" she asked.

"He is an asset, a contact, and a valuable one. He cares more for himself than for causes, and loves peace better than war. It enables him to enjoy all that he has more freely."

"Do you pay him for information or help?"

"Sometimes, sometimes not. It depends on the cause and the generosity of his spirit on any given day. And, like any good businessman, he knows that occasionally doing something nice for those he works with reaps him greater rewards in the future."

"Sounds...interesting."

"Only answer if he speaks to you directly, and, as always, be discreet in those answers."

"I understand," she said. "If you have this relationship, whatever it is, with him, then why are we still going disguised as a German businessman and his wife?"

"So as not to draw too much attention from anyone else. It is well known that Omar does business with many people throughout Europe. Our arriving to pay our respects to him and his daughter will not be seen as strange. On the other hand, an Israeli and an American arriving at his home at any time would be marked with suspicion."

It was a strange world that Jeremiah had brought her into, but she was determined to do her best to keep up appearances and not break their cover.

When Jeremiah left that night she tried to go to sleep, but found herself tossing and turning, fearful in this new place and worried about what might be happening to him. She hadn't wanted to leave his side until they were back home, but the look on his face when he'd told her couldn't take her that night had been convincing.

It was nearly six in the morning when he finally returned. She pretended to be asleep. In the morning he told her that he hadn't been able to find the man he was looking for. He would try again that night if he didn't get the information he needed from Omar at the wedding reception.

The next afternoon Cindy felt like she had stepped into an entirely different world. Tents were set up all around the grounds of a prestigious looking home. Everywhere she looked she saw musicians, dancers, and other revelers. The largest tent covered over banquet tables where hundreds were beginning to be seated.

Jeremiah had purposely timed their arrival for right after the wedding ceremony so as not to intrude on the bride and groom's most sacred moment. It was very thoughtful of him, she thought, and it showed a respect for the man they were going to see.

The air was filled with the scents of fresh bread, mint, and sweet smells that tantalized her. Everywhere she saw people making merry as you would expect at a reception. However it was larger and far more elaborate than even Geanie and Joseph's had been. She glimpsed the bride, wearing white, beaming at a young man next to her. She looked happy and it made Cindy smile. It also filled her heart for a moment with longing.

Jeremiah approached a servant and whispered something to the man. He disappeared and then reappeared a minute later and gestured for them to follow. Jeremiah gave her his arm as they entered into the house.

They swept through a grand entryway and then turned to the left where there was a sitting room with opulent wall decorations and dozens of colorful cushions scattered around the floor.

There was no one there, and they turned, facing the door, waiting. Moments later a large man entered.

"Now, who is it that disturbs my celebrations?" the man asked. He stopped short when he saw Jeremiah. Then slowly he moved forward until he was standing in front of him. This had to be Omar, Cindy realized.

"I had never thought to see your face again," Omar said.

"As they say, 'visit rarely and you will be more loved'," Jeremiah responded.

Omar laughed, "In that case you must have stayed away a hundred years by my count. That is how much love I have for you."

He embraced Jeremiah, his face jovial. "Welcome, my friend. It has been too long." Omar's eyes drifted to Cindy. "Do my eyes deceive me or have you taken yourself a wife at last?"

"I have," Jeremiah said, tightening his arm protectively around her waist.

"And here I thought a man such as you was cursed to be always alone."

"You know the thing I've learned about curses? Most of them can be broken."

Jeremiah's tone was light-hearted, but she could feel the tension in the arm that was around her waist. He was anything but relaxed. Still, she forced herself to smile.

"Omar, this is my wife, Cindy," Jeremiah said.

Omar took her hand in his. "A god-given beauty needs no beautician, my dear, and that certainly applies to you."

"Thank you," she said.

"Welcome to my home."

A figure darkened the doorway.

"What do you want? Can't you see I'm with friends?" Omar roared.

"Your wife needs you."

Omar sighed. "I shall return shortly. And then, we shall talk. Until then, please make yourselves comfortable. Eat! You look hungry, and hunger is the infidel."

He exited the room and Cindy turned to Jeremiah. "He is interesting," she said.

Jeremiah nodded. He turned and began to walk around the room, eyes looking everywhere.

"Is everything okay?" she finally asked.

"I think so," he said as he returned to her side.

It was a new day and Mark had arrived at the hospital early, smuggling in Traci some donuts. The day before had gotten busy once he got back to the hospital. Several people had been by to visit including Amber and Doug who were overjoyed to see their niece and nephew. Traci's mom had called and talked for a while, reminding them that once the babies came from the hospital she would be coming for a two week visit to help. Mark was definitely not looking forward to that.

He had just handed Traci her second donut when his phone rang. He checked it and didn't recognize the number. He was about to put his phone away when Traci stopped him.

"Who is it?"

"I'm not sure. I'll check the voicemail later if they leave one."

"Answer it," she said, getting a strange look on her face. "Hurry."

Her expression frightened him and his hand slipped on the phone, but he managed to answer it before it went to voicemail.

"Hello, this is Detective Walters," he said.

"Oh, Detective, I'm glad you answered. This is Amy Smith, we talked yesterday."

"Yes, Amy, what can I do for you?" The girl sounded frightened.

"I have something I think you need to see."

"I can meet you at the coffee shop."

"No, I don't want to meet in public. Can you come to my apartment?"

"Sure. Just give me the address."

He quickly grabbed a piece of paper and a pen and wrote it down as she rattled it off. "Hurry, please," she said.

He hung up. "I just got the weirdest-"

"Go!" Traci shouted.

"What?" he asked, taken aback.

She was shaking. "I have the most awful feeling. You have to go right now. Please, hurry!" She started crying. His natural instinct was to step forward to comfort her, but mindful of her words he turned and ran. He sprinted down the corridor, bypassed the elevator and took the stairs two at a time. By the time he skidded into his car he was sweating and the hair on the back of his neck was standing on end. Traci's fear had communicated itself to him and he slammed the flashing light on top of his car and hit the siren as he peeled out of the parking lot.

Ten minutes later he was pounding on Amy's door.

She opened it, and he saw that she was shaking. Her face was blotchy, evidence that she had been crying. She stepped back and he walked in.

"What is it?" he snapped, searching the room for signs of danger. He couldn't see anything. Why had Traci wanted him to hurry?

Amy picked up a letter off the table and held it in her shaking hands. "I was thinking about our conversation. I realized I forgot to tell you that one of Asim's best friends was this homeless guy in the park. They used to sit together and talk, sometimes for hours. I never understood it, but I was always proud that he wasn't the type of person to judge."

The dead former C.I.A. agent had known Asim, Mark realized. He might have known far more about the student's death than even Mark had suspected.

Amy wasn't finished, though. "I kept thinking about what you said, about how I should let go of the guilt. I've kept this letter for two years. It arrived the day after he died. He sent it the morning of his death. I was always too ashamed, too afraid of what he might have said about us, the fight, to read it. I was scared. What you said, though, I realized I had to stop being scared and face the truth. I never opened it until just before I called you."

She held it out to him.

Mark took it from her fingers and began to read.

My Dearest Amy,

If you are reading this, then something has happened to me. I have given this letter to my friend, Peter, to mail if it does. I'm hoping I will just be able to tear it up and you'll never have to know how close I came to losing you. I am sorry about the fight we had. I couldn't tell you what was going on because I didn't want to get you involved. I should explain now.

When I went back to Iran for Tamir's wedding I found my brothers even more twisted by anger and hatred than when I left. I was dismayed at their current state. By accident I learned that they were planning something dreadful with a handful of others, an act of terror that would inevitably plunge the region into war. I tried to reason with them, and I thought I had succeeded.

A week ago my brother called me as you know. I'm sorry I couldn't talk to you at the time about the nature of the call. I discovered that I had not dissuaded them as I had hoped. He tried to convince me that theirs was a just cause, but I would not listen. He begged me to side with them and told me that they had powerful friends who would not broach a security leak.

It frightened me, but I stood firm. In desperation, I talked to Peter. I know that might seem strange, but the man once worked for the government. I asked for his help and he agreed to reach out to some former friends. He was worried, though, that they wouldn't believe him. I couldn't blame them. A homeless man with mental problems and an Iranian college student do not make the most trustworthy sources in the eyes of those with no imagination.

Then the Russian woman approached me. I do not know her name, but I do know that she is working with my brothers. She tried to persuade me again, but I stood firm. She told me she would give me until this morning to decide. I am going to the park to meet her. I pray that she is alone. If she is then perhaps I can overpower her. Maybe Peter can help. If I have her in custody maybe then someone will listen to what I have to say.

I am so sorry that we fought. I will make it up to you if I can, and if I cannot, please know that I loved you and was faithful only to you. My uncle knew about you and I had hoped in a few more months when you knew me even better to ask you to be my wife. I do not say this to make you feel bad, only to let you know how deeply you were loved.

Be happy, for my sake.

All my love,

Asim

Mark felt as though a knife were twisting in his gut. He reread the letter. He had been right to connect the dots that he had between Asim, Peter, and Jeremiah. Peter must have failed in convincing any of his old colleagues at the C.I.A. that there was a credible threat.

And then, in desperation, he turned to Jeremiah. He had known Jeremiah when the rabbi was still a Mossad agent. Maybe he'd hoped that Jeremiah would believe and be able to convince others where he had failed.

He looked up at Amy. "He did love you, and he'd want you to be happy."

She nodded.

"I need to make some calls. Will you be okay?"

She nodded again.

"Call if you need anything."

Mark left, heading quickly for his car. The call he needed to make he didn't want anyone else to overhear.

A few minutes later Omar reappeared. "I am sorry for keeping you."

"We are sorry for interrupting this day," Jeremiah said. "Let us be brief so you can go and celebrate more with your family."

"Alright," Omar said, seating himself on one of the cushions on the floor and indicating for them to do the same.

Jeremiah held onto Cindy's hand as she sat. Once she was comfortable he sat down beside her.

"You are right, of course, my daughter is missing my presence, though I am surprised she notices anything but her husband." He looked at Cindy. "Are all brides so giddy on their wedding days?"

Cindy smiled. "It is a good thing. Your daughter looked very happy."

Omar shrugged. "Tamir is not my first choice for a son-in-law. He is a recent widower. But, my daughter met him at school and she thinks the world of him, so."

He turned to Jeremiah. "What is it that I can do for you?"

Even though they were alone in the room she noticed that Jeremiah still leaned forward. "There are troubling rumors of an attack that is planned in Jerusalem."

Omar waved his hand in the air. "There are always rumors. Believe what you see and lay aside what you hear, that's what I always say."

"These rumors I cannot lay aside. The attack would be a great atrocity."

Omar dropped his eyes to his hands. "Do the rumors speak of which side will make this attack?"

"No."

"The wound that bleedeth inwardly is the most dangerous," Omar said.

"You believe it to be my countrymen?" Jeremiah asked sharply.

"As they say, the wrath of brothers is fierce and devilish."

"Please, help me. Tell me what you know, or, at least, what you have heard."

Omar looked up at him and there was conflict in his eyes. "They say a foolish man may be known by six things. The second is speech without profit."

"I can make sure you profit for your speech," Jeremiah said, narrowing his eyes.

"I'm afraid that sometimes even gold cannot save a man. I always say, do not stand in a place of danger trusting in miracles."

Cindy realized he was afraid to tell them what he knew. She glanced at Jeremiah, wondering how he would persuade the other man to help them.

"If you know what I am speaking of then you know the consequences. It is said that a person who does not speak out against the wrong is a mute devil."

Suddenly Jeremiah's cell phone rang, startling Cindy. He reached for it to silence it, but then his hand hesitated above the screen.

"What is it?" she asked.

"The detective is calling," he said.

"Take your call, my friend, it will give me a moment to ponder your words," Omar said with a wave of his hand.

Out of habit Jeremiah rarely kept numbers stored in his phone. He still memorized numbers as it kept the information safer. He had recognized Mark's number and knew that Mark wouldn't be calling unless something serious had happened. Jeremiah's gut told him he needed to take the call. He answered it and stood swiftly, walking several paces away from Omar so the other man couldn't overhear what he had to say. Out of habit he turned his head away in case the other man could read lips.

"What is it?" Jeremiah asked tersely.

"I've done some more digging. I'm convinced that the Iranian student that was killed here two years ago found out about an impending terrorist plot that his two brothers were involved in, and that he was killed, likely by a Russian woman, before he could tip off the authorities. My gut is telling me this has something to do with the reason you're over there."

He heard the rustling of cloth and he wondered if Cindy was getting up to come check on him and find out what was up with Mark.

"Do you have names?"

"Yes. The last name is Kazmi. The oldest brother, Khalid, moved to Jerusalem six months ago. The other brother is still in Iran. His name is Tamir."

Jeremiah spun on his heel, his left hand reaching for his knife. Then he froze as he saw what had made the rustling noise behind him. Omar had his hand over Cindy's mouth and a gun at her temple.

14

Cindy was terrified. She could feel the steel of the gun against her temple. Omar had moved so quickly she hadn't had time to scream and warn Jeremiah. One moment he had been smiling at her, telling her he liked her dress and the next he had turned on them.

He whistled and several armed men ran into the room. Jeremiah removed his hand very slowly from the back of his waistband and raised it into the air. He raised his right as well which still held the cell phone.

"Take his weapon and tie him up," Omar ordered.

Jeremiah stared at Omar, his eyes dark. "I did not bring a gun into your home, Omar, but I will be leaving it with one."

Cindy could hear amusement in Omar's voice as he answered, "You forgot one of the most important sayings my friend. 'Think of the going out before you enter.' You did not have an exit strategy."

"I forgot a far more important proverb," Jeremiah said. "'Be careful of your enemy once and of your friend a thousand times, for a double crossing friend knows more evil.'"

"That is one I never forget," Omar said.

The guards swarmed Jeremiah and after a minute bound his arms behind him. When they were finished, Omar eased the gun away from her temple and took his hand from her mouth. A guard moved close and handed Omar Jeremiah's phone which he secreted in his clothes.

Jeremiah locked eyes with her. "Whatever happens, wife, I want you to never forget I love you. Estás mi corazón."

Cindy blinked. Jeremiah had called her his heart in Spanish. There had to be a reason for it.

"Estás mi corazón, también," she told him. She'd taken Spanish in high school. She was sure she'd probably told him that at some point. She guessed he was gambling it was a language no one else in the room would know.

"Cuando diré la palabra amigo en Inglés, harás lo qué hiciste a Aaron."

She understood well enough what he was trying to say. She was afraid that Omar would be suspicious that they were plotting their escape together, so she answered in English, "I will always take care of our Aaron, just as I have done in the past."

Nobody else said anything, so Jeremiah must have been right to think that she was the only one who knew any Spanish.

Jeremiah had made himself perfectly clear to her, at least. While Omar was holding a gun on her Jeremiah would not act. So, she had to be the one to change the balance of power. She just had to wait for his signal.

"Get up slowly, my dear," Omar said. "We're all going for a little walk."

When the call abruptly cut off Mark stared at the phone in horror. He had just heard Jeremiah and Cindy captured. Even as he sat there staring at his phone whoever had them might be killing them. The worst part was there was no one he could call to go rescue them. Even if he knew where to begin he had no idea where they were. He felt even more helpless than when he had tortured a man only to discover that he couldn't do what Mark needed him to even if he had wanted.

He called Traci. His voice was cracking as he explained to her what had happened. "Call Geanie and Joseph and tell them what's happening," Traci barked. "I've got something to do."

"What?" he asked, dazed.

"I'm going to do for Cindy what she'd do for me. I'm going to pray."

Omar had led them deeper into the house where, in his words, they would not be disturbed.

Jeremiah was angry that he had allowed himself to be betrayed like that. Fortunately his small, plastic knife had been easy to slip sidewise under his waistband and had gone unnoticed by Omar's men. It was sharp enough to cut through his ropes if he just had a few seconds where he wasn't being too closely observed.

Once they made it into the room that Omar had chosen two of his guards remained at the door. The others he dismissed saying, "This one usually works alone, but check the perimeter. We don't want any more uninvited guests."

Omar settled himself down on a chair so large it might as well have been a throne. He motioned for Cindy to sit on one of the cushions and she reluctantly did. He motioned to another one indicating that Jeremiah should sit.

"No, thank you. I prefer to stand in the presence of my enemies."

"I am sorry that you think of me as such," Omar said, still keeping the gun in his hand and pointed at Jeremiah.

"How could I not? What happened to you, Omar? You used to be a smart man who preferred peace and a good bargain."

"You have been gone a long time, Malachi. Things change."

"Not that much. You've always been more businessman than zealot."

"Perhaps my new son-in-law persuaded me otherwise."

"I don't believe it," Jeremiah said. He shifted his weight to cover for the fact that his fingers were grasping at the knife.

Omar chuckled. "You have always known me well. Let's just say that I have found a new business arrangement, a thousand times more profitable than any of the old ones."

"But it requires a war," Jeremiah guessed. "So, I know the Iranian players. Why not tell me who the Israeli betrayers are."

"You know, I would be tempted to, but I do not know their names," Omar said.

Unfortunately Jeremiah believed him.

"Besides," Omar continued. "Names would be no good to a dead man."

Jeremiah slowly, steadily with tiny movements was sawing through the ropes that bound his wrists. He had flexed all the muscles in his arm to allow himself some extra give in his restraints when he relaxed. "Well, since I am a dead man, humor me and tell me more about the Russians' involvement."

Omar's smile faded. "How could you know about that?"

"Simple, one of your Russian friends was sloppy and left a whole lot of evidence behind when she killed your son-in-law's brother."

Omar shook his head. "You are mistaken. I spoke with him on the phone not one hour ago."

"Khalid, yes. I'm talking about the other brother, the one who was killed in America because he refused to go along with the plot to blow up Qubbat As-Sakhrah."

Omar glared at him. "You know more than I expected."

Jeremiah smiled. "And you know less. You didn't even know about the other brother, did you? What other things are your partners keeping from you? Has to make you wonder. In fact, once they've accomplished their purpose, why will they need you at all?"

"That's enough!" Omar shouted, standing suddenly.

The last strand gave way and Jeremiah held onto the rope to keep it from falling.

"You referred to a proverb earlier that I think actually does fit you in this situation. They say that 'a foolish man may be known by six things: anger without cause, speech without profit, change without progress, inquiry without object, putting trust in a stranger," Jeremiah paused and met Cindy's eyes before finishing, "and mistaking foes for friends."

Cindy lunged to her feet and hit Omar's hand so hard that the gun went flying. Jeremiah hurled the knife and it found its mark in one of the guard's throats. Cindy dove across the floor and managed to wrap her hands around the gun.

The remaining guard fired off a single wild shot before Jeremiah slammed into him, carrying him to the floor. He sat up and snapped the man's neck before scrambling to Cindy and taking the gun from her shaking hand. "That's my girl," he whispered encouragingly. She had done perfectly, but he needed her to keep it together and not fall apart yet.

Omar raised his hands into the air. "But, Malachi, you must know I wouldn't have harmed you, we have been friends too long."

"Beware of he whose goodness you can't ask for and whose evil you can't be protected from," Jeremiah growled. "You will get us out of here, now."

"Yes, of course. I have a secret exit. I put it in years ago."

"One word to alert anyone and I will kill you. Do you understand?"

Omar nodded. He had begun to perspire and he reeked of fear. He led them out of the room, down a hall, and then into a bedroom. Jeremiah's eyes fell on some clothes sitting on a chest. He looked at Cindy and nodded at them. She scooped up a handful and tucked them under her arm. Omar moved to the back wall of the room and there he opened a secret panel to reveal a long, dark tunnel.

"Through here and you will be safe," Omar said.

Jeremiah shook his head. "You'll be going with us."

"I promise you, this will lead to the outside."

"And I promise you that when we get to the end of it, if I so much as see one of your men you will breathe your last. You go first. Cindy, walk behind me."

Omar entered the tunnel, whimpering in his throat. There was a lantern which he lit as Jeremiah closed the section of wall behind them. "There is no going back," Jeremiah said, "only forward."

He was speaking as much to Cindy as he was to Omar.

He felt her hand rest lightly on his shoulder. He welcomed it since then he knew exactly where she was without having to take his eyes off Omar.

The tunnel went on for at least half a mile. He could hear Cindy's breathing becoming more rapid and shallow toward the end. She was becoming fearful in the closed, cramped space.

"You did a fantastic job back there, Cindy, just as I asked," he said to get her mind off her burgeoning claustrophobia.

"Thank you," she said.

"Bet you never thought you'd be using your high school Spanish for that."

"No, I never would have guessed in a million years."

"You'll have to look up your old teacher when we get back home and thank them, tell them that Spanish saved your life. I bet that's one thing they'll never have heard."

"I can imagine that would come as quite a shock," she said.

He could tell that the distraction was working. Her breathing was steadying out. Omar's, on the other hand, had started to become erratic. Either he was planning to try something or they were approaching the end of the tunnel.

"Steady, Omar," he said.

"We are almost there," Omar said.

"Good. Remember, if I see anything I don't like-"

"I know," Omar said, interrupting him.

"As long as we're clear on that."

A dozen more steps and they came to a wall. Omar hung the lantern on a hook nearby. Then he pressed a section of the wall and it moved, sliding open to reveal a Tehran alleyway. The sun was setting in the sky, painting it in colors of fire. It was brilliantly bright after the darkness of the tunnel.

The alley appeared to be deserted.

"You first, Omar," Jeremiah said.

The other man nodded and then stepped out into the alleyway. Jeremiah followed with Cindy pushing into him in her eagerness to be free of the darkness of the tunnel.

"Now, please, go," Omar pleaded.

Jeremiah shook his head. "As you noted Omar, I've been gone a while. I don't know the city anymore. Not like you do. You need to get us farther away where no one will find us."

Omar nodded slowly.

"And make sure to keep us out of sight," Jeremiah said. He looked at Cindy. "What did you find?"

"A woman's skirt and blouse and a man's shirt," she said, still holding the clothes she had taken from the house.

"Do you have your scarf in your pocket still?"

She nodded.

"Good, put the clothes on, quickly, and cover your head."

To her credit she did so in less than a minute, pulling the skirt and shirt on over what she was already wearing.

"Seal up the tunnel," Jeremiah ordered and Omar complied as Jeremiah carefully slipped into the shirt Cindy handed him.

"Okay, now we go," Jeremiah said.

Omar led the way and he managed to keep them out of sight as they wove through various streets. At last Jeremiah felt he was in familiar territory toward the western edge of the city.

"In there, that will be safe for the moment," Jeremiah said, indicating an abandoned building that was crumbling into ruins.

Omar stepped inside, pushing away a door that was sagging off its hinges. Jeremiah and Cindy followed.

"You know where you are now, yes?" Omar asked.

"I do," Jeremiah said. "Now, on your knees."

The man hastily dropped to his knees, his whole attitude that of a penitent begging forgiveness.

"My friend, I am so sorry. I've been trapped in this plot, unable to get out. A victim myself," Omar babbled. "Please, I'm begging you to have mercy."

Jeremiah lifted the gun and the man started crying softly.

"What are you doing?" Cindy asked, fear in her voice.

"I can't let him go. He knows who we are."

He glanced at Cindy. Her eyes were wide in terror and she was shaking. It was the moment of truth, the one he'd been dreading for so long.

"Do you know what I did for a living before I was a rabbi?"

"You were a spy."

"No."

He shot Omar twice in the head. As his body fell Jeremiah turned back to her. "I was an assassin."

156

15

Cindy couldn't take her eyes off Omar's body. Jeremiah had killed him. He'd never had any intention of letting him go. She understood why, knew that he had betrayed Jeremiah and her and could not be trusted. He was also plotting to unleash evil on the world.

But she was still in shock. Maybe it was the brutality of it. Maybe it was the fact that Omar had been unarmed and helpless. She took a deep breath. *Jeremiah executed him.*

Cindy knew Jeremiah had killed people. She'd even suspected that it had been a lot of people, but she hadn't known that was his primary job for the Mossad. That was one thing he hadn't shared. Yet knowing that made everything else make sense, particularly his fear of getting pulled back into his old life. All that flashed through her mind, but she didn't say anything as he took her hand and pulled her toward the door after he had grabbed a phone off Omar's body.

"We're going to have to hit some busier streets. Stay right with me and keep your eyes on the ground. Don't make eye contact with anyone and don't speak," he said.

She nodded, not sure what she'd even say at the moment. Her heart was in her throat and she was still in shock.

They moved fast, running down alleyways, speed walking down streets where there were people present. She stayed so close to Jeremiah that their arms were frequently in contact. It seemed like they had to have traversed half the city by the time he pulled them into a dark alley beside another abandoned building.

"We'll rest here for a little while, catch our breath," Jeremiah said.

She realized that had to be for her benefit because he didn't even seem to have broken a sweat and yet she was panting like an animal.

He squatted down but he didn't relax. She could see the tightness in all his muscles. He was constantly swiveling his head, eyes roving everywhere as he looked for danger.

"Now you know everything," he said after a minute, startling her. He didn't look at her and she couldn't pick up on his emotions from his voice which had sounded cold, detached.

"Not quite everything. Why did you decide to retire?" she asked when she could breathe normally enough to get the words out.

"I didn't. They forced me to retire," he said.

"Why? I would think they would always need people with your...skills," she said, thinking about how Solomon and he had danced around his job experience using that same word when talking in front of her.

"They also need people who follow orders," he said.

"Did you refuse to kill someone they told you to?" she asked.

He turned and looked at her and gave a short, harsh laugh. Then he shook his head. "That would make everything easier to accept, I'm sure. But that's not the case."

"Then why did they force you to retire?"

He turned away, resuming his relentless scanning of the area. "I was sent to a high level meeting of a terrorist cell that was involved in everything from bombings to human trafficking. My orders were to kill one man, the second highest ranking member of the cell that was present. I spent a day setting up for it, preparing. And then it came time to do it."

"What happened?" she asked when he paused.

He sighed, but continued. "I thought to myself that who knew when we'd have this opportunity again. There were ten men there, and I killed all of them."

Cindy sat very still, listening, trying to take it in. Her mind was conjuring up images that she didn't like, extrapolating based on the things she had actually seen Jeremiah do.

"Two hours later I'm face-to-face with my handler. I never knew the man could move that fast. He was furious, demanded to know why I hadn't followed orders. I reminded him that he chose me because of my ability to make decisions in the blink of an eye and to adapt to changing circumstances. He asked what had changed about the entire operation that I'd ended up killing everyone. I told him nothing had changed with the operation, but that I'd realized there was no reason to let even one of those men go free. Then he gave me a reason, a good one. They had managed to turn one of the cell members. The man had recently had a child giving him a newfound respect for life and a sudden, healthy fear of his compatriots. When I shot the number two guy he was going to play the hero and save the life of the number one guy at that meeting, thus earning his trust. You see, all those men were evil men, but my bosses had a plan to try and get to the real head of the organization, a man who had not shown his face in public in ten years. The turncoat was their way in. And with ten well-placed shots instead of one, I destroyed months of work and their one chance at getting that guy."

"And that's why they forced you to retire?" she asked softly.

"Actually, no. Agents blunder. It happens. They were looking at some vacation time for me so I could get my head straight. Instead they forced me to retire because I told them that even given all the new information, I'd still kill those ten men again regardless of the consequences. Everyone of them deserved to die and I didn't have the stomach to let them go for any reason. My handler knew he could never again trust me to follow an order."

"Given what you had done I'm surprised they just let you retire."

"Solomon was angry enough to kill me that day. I understood. Instead, though, he sent me to America, had me retrained, and set me up with a new identity and a new life."

"But why?"

"Because he knew that someday he might need someone who wouldn't follow orders."

They needed to get out of the city, but they were going to need help. They couldn't go back to the hotel and their fake passports were locked up in its safe so even if they made it to the airport they'd have a devil of a time getting on a plane.

Jeremiah pulled out his cell phone. He couldn't risk having Solomon send someone to help them. There had to be a leak somewhere in his inner circle else how would the enemy have known when he sent someone to California to get Jeremiah?

There was only one man that might be able to help, but it was a long shot. He called Martin.

"Hello?" the man answered.

"It's your cousin the rabbi. I'm needing a favor worse than I did the other day."

"Unless you're a long way from the States there's nothing I can do to help you at the moment," the man said tersely.

"Lucky for both of us I'm not. I have information you need."

"What kind of information?" Martin asked cautiously.

"I know who's going after the Rock," Jeremiah said, unwilling to say more on an open line. He didn't know for sure who all was involved but he did have some names to pass on and a dead conspirator.

"Tell me."

"First, I need an extraction for me and a certain young lady."

"You brought her into this?" Martin hissed.

"Really didn't have a choice. An associate was too busy to do me a favor," Jeremiah said, letting sarcasm drip from his tongue.

Martin swore. "Okay, where are you?"

"Tehran."

More swearing. "Care to be more specific?"

Jeremiah gave him their location. It was risky, but he needed the help.

"Alright, I'll be sending some men to get you in fifteen minutes. Sit tight, and don't shoot. I'll be the guy in front."

Martin ended the call and Jeremiah turned to Cindy. "Help is on the way."

"Okay."

He tried not to look at her. He could hear the pain and fear in her voice. He knew she was physically spent. What he was afraid of, though, was looking at her and seeing condemnation in her eyes. It would destroy him, and before he could let that happen he had to stop the terror plot. Then he would make sure that Cindy made it back home safely and if she hated him, feared him as he believed she must then he would leave her alone forever.

Cindy was exhausted both mentally and physically. More than all the activity, the stress was what was wearing her down. Her body wasn't used to the constant onslaught of anxiety and adrenalin. In the last few years she'd experienced similar things but not so sustained with so little rest for so long. She had no idea how Jeremiah had managed to make a career out of this.

Jeremiah had said that help was on the way. She didn't know who he had called, but she would be grateful to anyone who could get them out of there.

His story was upsetting, but she understood so much more now that she knew it. She couldn't blame him for his desire to kill the entire terrorist group who was responsible for so much death and human misery. He'd said they'd even been responsible for human trafficking which just made her sick to the bottom of her soul. She was glad they were dead. She just wished that the rest who participated in such abominations were as well.

"Why did Mark call?" she asked.

"He discovered who killed the student a couple of years ago. Turns out the boy's brothers were involved in some sort of terrorist plot and he was pretty sure it was connected to what we were investigating. It is."

"How do you know?"

"The brothers are named Khalid and Tamir."

"Tamir? As in the man who just married Omar's daughter?"

"It looks like it. If Mark had called just five minutes earlier things would be a lot different right now."

"Yes, they could be even worse," Cindy pointed out.

She thought about Omar's daughter. She wondered if the woman knew she was marrying a terrorist or if she had known what her husband and her father were up to. Cindy hoped she did. It was easier to think about her that way than to think about her as young, naive, unwittingly in love with the wrong man, and about to find out that her father had been killed on her wedding day. She didn't want it to be that complicated. She wanted it to be simple. She wanted the woman to have known exactly what she was getting herself into so she would know exactly why her father had died and her husband had to as well.

"Are you okay?" Jeremiah asked.

She wasn't sure how to answer that. Finally with a sigh she said, "No, but I will be. Right now I just want to get out of here."

Jeremiah stood and she could see the gun in his hand. "Hopefully this is our ride," he said.

"Someone's coming?" she asked, scrambling to her feet.

He nodded silently.

It took almost half a minute more but she finally heard footsteps. Her heart began to hammer in her chest as she wondered if they belonged to friend or foe. She kept her eyes fixed on the corner closest to them. She could sense people just around the bend, out of sight.

"Rabbi, don't shoot," a voice said softly.

She glanced at Jeremiah. He was standing slightly sideways, and he had the gun raised.

A moment later a man cautiously rounded the corner. He also had a gun raised. Cindy blinked. She recognized him, but it took her a moment to realize from where.

"Martin?" she asked, bewildered.

"Just your friendly, neighborhood salesman. Anyone here need some medical supplies?"

Relief washed over her. Jeremiah had told her that the man worked for the C.I.A.

Three more men slowly rounded the corner, all with guns drawn.

"Everything okay, rabbi?" Martin asked.

"They'd be better if you and your men put down your guns," Jeremiah said evenly.

"How about you go first?" Martin suggested.

"Not going to happen."

"Hey, you called me, remember?" Martin said.

"I did. I'm still trying to decide if that was the smart move."

"What's going on?" Cindy asked as the relief she had been feeling quickly faded.

"Just trying to establish what side everyone's on," Martin said.

"You have me outnumbered. I'm at the disadvantage," Jeremiah said.

"That's bull, and you know it, rabbi."

"How do you figure?"

"Right before you called I had an interesting chat with one of my counterparts from Israel. He told me that a retired operative was back and had gone rogue."

"If that was true you'd already be dead," Jeremiah said evenly.

"Unless you needed me for something, say to get a certain lady to safety," Martin said.

"We're all on the same side," Cindy protested. She wanted to scream at them, tell them they were all being idiots and that they needed to work together because time was running out. She barely managed to control her tone of voice, though, knowing that anything more aggressive or startling could inadvertently cause someone to start shooting.

"Maybe, maybe not," Martin said.

"How do I know you're not lying about your information?" Jeremiah said. "You spent time over here. For all I know your sympathies were aroused."

"You didn't tell me who you were," Martin said.

"I never tell anyone who I am," Jeremiah hissed.

Cindy barely managed to stop herself from blurting out that what he had just said was most certainly true.

"And yet everyone knows of the great malakh ha-mavet. I just didn't know I had already met him. Pretty slick cover, pretending to be a rabbi."

"He's not pretending. He is a rabbi," Cindy hissed. She couldn't stand it anymore. While the clock ran out to stop the real terrorists they were in danger of being killed by the very people who should be helping them.

"Enough!" Cindy declared. She stepped forward deliberately, putting herself between Jeremiah and Martin.

"Get out of the way, Cindy," both men said at the same time.

"No, I won't. This is ridiculous. We have found out the names of a couple of the terrorists. Instead of distrusting each other we need to be working to fight them. From what I can tell there's probably a couple of Israelis working with them. One of them is most likely the person who told you that...the rabbi...was here."

"We also know there's at least one Russian involved."

"Where there's one Russian there's always more," Martin said.

"There's a rich man named Omar whose daughter got married today. Omar was one of the terrorists. Her husband, Tamir, is another one."

"Omar's body turned up just a few minutes ago. So, that's one down," Martin said.

"And you can thank us for that," Cindy said defiantly.

"'Us'?" Martin and Jeremiah echoed at the same time.

"Yes. Us," she said, glaring at Martin. "He had captured us and I helped us escape. After we found out what we could from him, well, then..." she ran out of steam, unable to finish the sentence. She could take partial credit for taking Omar hostage, but none for actually killing him. She was actually grateful for that. "I don't know if Tamir is still at the wedding reception."

"How many men do you have at your disposal?" Jeremiah asked.

Martin narrowed his eyes. "Enough to kill him if he's there, not enough to take him captive."

166

"His brother is another one of the conspirators, and he's already in Jerusalem," Jeremiah said.

"Which is where we should be heading next," Cindy added.

"The agent who warned you about me," Jeremiah said. "Who was it?"

"Sorry, rabbi. I can't take the risk of you killing him if you are on the wrong side and he's on the right one."

"This is ridiculous!" Cindy said, losing the fragile hold she had on her anger, which was pushing down her fear and pain, and taking hold of her.

"I'll do some digging, see if I can figure out on my own which side that agent is actually on."

"And what will you do until then? He will be suspicious if you have not followed his advice and he could accelerate the timetable for the explosion or come after you," Jeremiah pointed out.

Martin nodded. "You have a valid point. So, there's only one solution I can think of."

"What's that?" Cindy asked.

"The rabbi can't leave this alley alive."

16

"I agree," Jeremiah said quietly.

"No!" Cindy screamed. She turned on Jeremiah who was lowering his gun and pounded on his chest with her fists. "What is wrong with you? You need to fight! You can't just give up!"

Jeremiah dropped the gun and put his arms around Cindy, pressing her head into his shoulder. "Listen to me, it's going to be okay."

All she could think over and over was that he had dropped his gun. Everything Martin had said, everything she had said hadn't been enough to get him to lower the weapon, but now he was surrendering, and not just to capture, but to death.

"Sometimes sacrifices have to be made," she heard Martin say.

"It's not worth it!" Cindy screamed, writhing against Jeremiah's chest. "I'd rather the whole world burned than lose you."

She felt him kiss the top of her head. "It's for the best," he whispered.

"I'll personally take your body back home," she heard Martin say. "It's the least I can do."

"Promise you'll get her to safety."

"I promise," Martin said.

She pushed off Jeremiah, turning to Martin. "Don't you touch him!" she screamed.

Martin gave her the strangest look. He opened his mouth as though to say something, but Jeremiah cut him off, his voice tense. "Martin, I don't want her to see this."

"Understood," Martin said. He nodded and two of the men with him holstered their weapons and stepped forward, each grabbing Cindy by an arm.

"No!" she screamed, fighting, clawing, and kicking at them.

They picked her up and carried her to the corner. She managed to kick one in the knee and he half dropped her. The third man with Martin also holstered his gun and grabbed hold of her. She twisted around just before they turned it and saw Jeremiah slowly kneeling on the ground. Martin had his gun aimed at his chest.

She screamed and one of the men holding her clamped his hand down on her mouth. She tried to bite him, but he was wearing gloves and it had no effect on him. She tried jabbing her fingers in his throat, but he twisted out of her reach. Her mind was reeling. She had to find a way to get free. She had to find a way to save Jeremiah. She had to-

She heard three shots followed a moment later by a thud as of a body hitting the ground.

She stopped struggling. Maybe Jeremiah had been clever. Maybe he had turned the tables on Martin. He had dropped his gun earlier, had it been near to where he was kneeling when she last saw him?

She heard footsteps and she twisted around, ready to do what she could to help Jeremiah overcome the three men who were holding her. Martin appeared around the corner, his face grim. He saw her and quickly put his gun away. He looked pained as he stared at her.

"Cindy, my condolences on your loss."

Her heart stopped and she closed her eyes as her entire body went limp. It wasn't true. It couldn't be.

"I think she fainted," she heard one of the men say.

"Give her some air," another said.

A moment later she felt herself being lowered onto the ground.

"This is a hell of a mess," Martin muttered.

It couldn't be true. She refused to believe that Jeremiah was dead. He had escaped, he had run and Martin had fired at him and missed. Jeremiah would come for her, rescue her like he always did.

She opened her eyes, flipped onto her stomach and had pushed up to her feet before they knew what had happened. She heard one of the men shout in surprise. She rounded the corner expecting to see an empty alley.

She stumbled as she saw a dark form lying on the ground.

"No," she whispered.

She felt hands reaching for her and she shook herself hard before racing forward. She tripped and landed on the ground next to Jeremiah. There were three bullet holes in his shirt, two near his heart and the other over his stomach. Each one was surrounded by fresh blood. The smell of it filled her nostrils.

His eyes were closed and he wasn't breathing. He truly was dead.

"No!" she screamed, reaching out to touch his face.

Then Martin had his arms around her and was pulling her away. "He didn't want you to see this," he said, his voice tinged with anger.

"You killed him," she sobbed.

"I did what I had to do."

She spun around to face him. "You're a murderer!"

He took a deep breath. "In this line of work, sooner or later we all are."

She was going to tear him limb from limb, but something was happening to her. She felt cold as ice and she felt like she could barely lift her arm. Her legs started to give out beneath her and Martin kept her from falling.

As if from a long ways away she heard him swear followed by the words, "She's going into shock."

Jeremiah was dead. That was all that she knew.

"We need to move the body," she heard Martin say.

How could Jeremiah have let Martin kill him? How could he have left her alone? Her thoughts descended further and further into darkness until all she felt was dull, aching pain.

Cindy was only dimly aware of the passing of the next several hours. Sometimes it seemed as though she were walking, other times it felt as though she was being carried. She was in a car for a while then everything was hazy.

Slowly she began to come back to her senses only to discover that she was on a plane. It wasn't a normal airline plane, though, it had to be a private one she realized. Cindy looked around and saw Martin seated across the aisle. A myriad of emotions washed over her.

"You killed him," she whispered.

Martin looked up from the papers he was studying. He looked at her and she saw a hint of guilt in his eyes. That was more than Jeremiah had shown for killing Omar. But Omar had been the enemy and Jeremiah had not.

"Why?"

Martin cleared his throat and put down his papers. "Cindy, this is a brutal business. Sometimes to save the lives of thousands you have to take the life of one."

"Jeremiah had nothing to do with these terrorist attacks. The Mossad forced him to come back here and help."

"I know."

"Then why?"

"Because we're not just talking about the lives of thousands. We're talking about millions. Our enemies clearly wanted Jeremiah dead. Now that I have a better idea of who they are hopefully I can get close enough to them to stop this terror attack from happening. Jeremiah understood that our enemies would never trust me to let me that close if I didn't kill him. He spent years in this business. He'd pulled the trigger on a lot of men, some deserved it, others, maybe not. He killed men that under any other circumstances he might have called friend."

Omar's pleading face flashed unbidden into Cindy's mind. She shoved the thought out angrily.

"He was one of the good guys."

Martin leaned toward her and there was real pain in his eyes. "I know. You think bad guys are the only ones who get killed? Jeremiah was one of the good guys. One of the best. That's why he was willing to sacrifice himself to save you, me, everybody. Only a noble man is capable of that kind of sacrifice."

"Greater love hath no man than this, that he lay down his life for his friends," Cindy whispered, quoting from the Bible.

"He could have shot at me and forced me to shoot back, but that would have potentially put you in danger and it would have left me doubting the truth of what he told me.

Laying down his gun, offering himself up like that was the most courageous thing he could have done." Martin sighed and rubbed his eyes. "I didn't want this. I wish that you weren't having to go through this agony. It's not fair, I know. You should understand one thing. It's the only bit of comfort I can offer you. I only ever spoke with him a handful of times, and I didn't know until...the end...exactly who he was, but one thing I knew from the first moment I laid eyes on him."

"What's that?" Cindy asked.

"He loved you more than anything. His only wish was for you to be safe and happy. In the end, that's what he gave his life for. If you would honor that, then when you get home, try to find some happiness for yourself."

"How can I be happy when the only thing I ever wanted has been taken from me?" she asked, tears spilling down her cheeks.

"I don't know," Martin said softly. He turned back to his papers and Cindy pressed her head back against the seat.

She couldn't stop the tears that flowed freely down her face anymore than she could stop the pain that was tearing her apart. And over and over she just kept realizing what a fool she had been to never tell him that she loved him, to never reach out and kiss him. All those hours spent together and yet now they were misspent, because he was gone and he'd never know how she felt and she'd never have the opportunity to kiss him.

She knew that even if she lived to be a hundred she'd never love again. She also knew that she would be the first to urge others to act on their feelings and express them. Even if Jeremiah had rejected her love the pain would have been nothing compared to the pain of losing him without ever truly having him.

She was dimly aware that the plane had begun to descend. Martin began to put all his papers away in a briefcase. When the wheels touched down she turned to look at him.

"Where are we?" she asked.

"Jerusalem."

"Why?"

"I promised him I'd bring his body home. And this is his home," he said.

She wanted to protest, to tell him that Jeremiah's home was in Pine Springs, California. She wanted him buried there where she could make sure they kept fresh flowers on his grave and she could visit from time to time.

She hung her head. She knew he had a family. She didn't know anything more about them than that. They'd want him to be buried here where his other relatives would be buried. Now that he was dead, surely he could go home to them.

Tears threatened to fall, but she wouldn't let them. She needed to get through whatever was coming next.

"What happens to me?" she asked.

"I'm going to make sure you make it back to California where you'll be safe," Martin said.

"Then the joke's on you. I won't be safe there. Jeremiah has enemies from his past there that will kill me just to try and get at him, never realizing that they can't get at him anymore."

Martin cleared his throat. "I feel partly responsible for the situation you're in. I'll do what I can to see that you are left alone."

174

Alone, that's exactly what she was.

"What about the shrine? We still have to stop the attack."

"Trust me, lots of people are working on that. You don't need to be one of them. You're not a professional, Cindy. It's best you go home."

"I saved Jeremiah's life on the plane ride to Tel Aviv," she said as the plane continued to taxi.

"Excuse me?"

"They'd sent a man to kill him. He drugged Jeremiah and was going to poison him, but I caught him in time. I stopped him and Jeremiah woke up just in time to kill him with his own poison. I wasn't a professional, but he needed me then. And, as much as I don't want to look at you ever again, I think you're going to need me, too."

She knew she must sound crazy, and she could scarcely believe the words that she was saying herself. She was the one who had always hidden from danger, fleeing it at every opportunity, avoiding risk whenever possible. Jeremiah had changed that for her. And if he had sacrificed his life to stop this terror attack then she saw no better way that she could honor him and his sacrifice than by sticking around to see his work through. She could do that for him, at least. If she was killed in the process then God would have spared her a lifetime of living without the man she loved.

"We've got more than enough-"

"What you've got are turncoats on every side. Jeremiah used to be able to trust Omar and Omar betrayed him. One or more people inside the Mossad have betrayed him and are part of this plot. Who do you know other than me that you can trust without question?" she asked, her voice raising as she spoke.

She turned and locked eyes with him, defying him to say otherwise.

"Truthfully, noone."

"And given that you murdered the man I love, what does that tell you?"

Martin took a deep breath. "That I'm in a whole lot of trouble."

"Exactly. I'm not leaving until this thing is finished."

"I'm afraid that's going to cause no end of problems."

"Deal with it," Cindy said before turning away.

She gripped the armrests of her seat, wishing that she could tear through them with her bare hands. One way or another she would see Jeremiah's work through to the end.

"I didn't know the two of you had gotten married," Martin said, glancing at the wedding ring she was still wearing.

"Just before we had to come here," she said, preserving the cover story. What did it matter now anyway? She felt like a widow, she might as well be treated like one.

"If you truly wish to help, then you need to back up the story I'll be telling once we get off the plane. No one can know that Jeremiah gave his life willingly or the reason why. Do you understand?"

"I do," she said through tight lips. "Don't worry about me." If there was one thing she'd learned on this trip it was how to lie.

The plane came to a stop at last. Martin unfastened his seatbelt and stood up and she did the same. She followed him to the front of the plane. A minute later they were descending down stairs onto the tarmac. At the bottom a couple of cars were waiting. One of them was a hearse. She nearly tripped on the stair when she saw it and her breath caught in her throat.

The doors to the first car opened and Solomon and his driver exited. She reached the bottom and walked over to the man who had been Jeremiah's handler. He reached out to her and took her hands and the pain in his eyes mirrored hers. "I am so sorry for your loss. It is never good to lose a husband, but to lose one so soon after having been married is unthinkable."

She didn't have to think of anything to say, she just nodded and let the tears that were flowing again speak for themselves. Solomon's eyes moved past her and she turned to see four men carrying Jeremiah's coffin off the plane.

17

Cindy's knees started to give way and Solomon caught her before she fell. Her head was spinning as she watched the coffin being carried to the back of the hearse. It wasn't a fancy coffin, the kind you'd see at funerals, but a rather plain wooden box. It seemed so hard to believe that it carried her heart inside it.

"Excuse me a moment," Solomon said, propping her up against his car. "Will you be alright?"

She managed to nod. He headed toward the hearse. After a moment she pushed off from the car and followed.

"You shouldn't look, it won't be pretty," Martin said, his face twisting in concern.

"I have to look."

She had seen Jeremiah's body in the alley, but even now that seemed like some hideous nightmare that was fading with the light. She had to see for herself.

She arrived behind the hearse just in time to hear Solomon order the men to open the coffin. She braced herself with a hand on the vehicle and placed her other over her heart.

She waited as the coffin lid opened and then crumpled over in pain. There was Jeremiah, his skin was a bluish-grey and the blood around the bullet holes in his chest had dried.

Solomon bowed his head. "Seal it back up," he said, his voice hoarse.

They did so and they placed the coffin in the back of the vehicle. She managed to pull herself back up to a standing position and she turned to see Martin staring at her with such compassion in his eyes that it physically hurt her to look at him. He had no right to look at her that way, not when he was the cause of her grief.

Solomon opened the back door of his car for Martin and Cindy and indicated that they should get inside. "We need to go somewhere to talk," he said.

Moments later they were inside the car and on their way. No one spoke during the ride which was just as well. Cindy had always wanted to see Jerusalem, but now she didn't even bother looking out the window.

She didn't know how much time passed but eventually the car stopped. The driver opened the door and they all got out. The hearse parked behind them. They were underground somewhere. Solomon led them to an elevator and after a short ride they emerged on a floor with no windows. Cindy figured they must still be underground.

A moment later they were all taking seats in a small conference room with dark paneling and a table that could seat six. Light was provided by four different wall sconces and a low hanging chandelier, shaped like the bottom half of a globe, which was over the table. Cindy fought the urge to put her head down on the table. The last time she'd gotten any sleep it had been back in Tel Aviv when she'd woken up beside Jeremiah. If only she could go back downstairs and shake him awake now.

If she was going to help, though, she needed to pay attention and focus.

"What happened?" Solomon asked without preamble.

"We were alerted to the fact that...Malachi... had killed his contact in Tehran. We're still trying to figure out why. By the time I reached him he was...unwilling to listen to reason. He refused to put down his weapon and he was talking nonsense about Russians recruiting Israeli and C.I.A. operatives. He killed two of my best men before I was able to take him down," Martin said gravely. He glanced at Cindy. "Unfortunately she saw the whole thing."

"Is this true?" Solomon asked Cindy.

She nodded and she did not have to fake the look of misery on her face. "I don't know what Omar said to him. They weren't speaking English. But Malachi just killed him, shot him twice in the head. The man was supposed to be his friend! He wasn't even carrying a weapon." She began to cry but kept going. "Then we were running for so long. He told me that he had lied to me about the work he did for you. He told me he was an assassin and that he hadn't quit because he wanted to be a rabbi. He told me that he wouldn't follow orders anymore and you fired him."

"Regrettably, this is all true," Solomon said, glancing from her to Martin. "He had a problem following orders at the end. I recalled him because of his knowledge, his contacts. Clearly that was my mistake."

"Why did he lie to me?" Cindy asked.

Solomon averted his eyes.

"My guess is that he was afraid of what you would think of him if you knew the truth," Martin said after a minute.

She nodded. She was struggling to keep in mind that she was acting a part on top of living a nightmare. Martin

180

needed her help right now, and if she was going to be a part of this thing then she needed his.

"That makes sense," she forced herself to say.

"We still have to stop the terrorists from completing their mission," Solomon said.

"Yes, we do," Martin said. "If you don't mind, though, I'd like to talk someplace a little less apt to be bugged."

"I can assure you that there are no listening devices in this room," Solomon said, bristling as though he had just been insulted.

"Really?" Martin asked, sarcasm thick in his voice. He stood up abruptly and grasped the tiny metal knob on the bottom of the chandelier. "Then what do you call this?" he asked.

He yanked it off and it fell a foot then dangled from a wire that was still attached to the chandelier.

Solomon cursed and leaped to his feet, hand reaching for his gun. Martin had his gun out first. "This is not my doing," Solomon hissed.

"Then we'd better move fast," Martin said. "Come on Cindy."

She staggered to her feet, stunned at the sudden revelation. She ran after them. They bypassed the elevator and hit a stairwell, and she scrambled to keep up as the men took the stairs at a breakneck pace. They burst into the parking garage and ran toward Solomon's car.

His driver got out. "Is something wrong?" the man asked.

"Everything's wrong," Solomon said.

"You have that right."

Several men emerged from the shadows, all pointing guns at them. Martin positioned himself in front of her.

Solomon's driver pulled a gun out of his jacket and he, too, trained it on them.

"You?" Solomon demanded, turning red.

The man shrugged, but did not say anything.

Martin looked at him. "You lying dog. You told me that Malachi had gone rogue."

"Thank you for believing it. When a friend in Tehran alerted me to his proximity I knew he was getting too close to uncovering our plan," the man said.

"You won't get away with this," Solomon said.

"Actually, by the time anyone sorts out what happened here it will all be over," the man said with a sneer.

Suddenly the entire parking garage was plunged into darkness. Martin reached out and pushed Cindy to the ground as the men started firing at them. "How many of them are there?" Martin hissed.

"Too many," someone else whispered.

A hand grabbed Cindy's arm and she struggled to see as she got to her feet. Then they were moving swiftly to the left. After a moment the shooting stopped.

"Find them!" someone ordered.

Now she could hear her own running steps and those of the men beside her. She just hoped that whoever had her arm knew where he was going. A few moments later her eyes perceived a dim light. It was a door. She pushed on it when she reached it and could see a dimly lit staircase leading upward. A hand in the middle of her back urged her forward and she ran as fast as she could.

The stairs seemed to go on forever in a straight line upward and her legs were slowing. She tripped and caught herself and pressed forward. Finally the stairwell appeared to be getting brighter and at last she could see a door above her. With a sob of relief she crashed through it a few seconds later and out onto a street.

She twisted her head left and right, looking for men with guns. She didn't see any. She had no idea where she was, but hopefully Solomon or Martin would know.

A hand on her shoulder steered her to run down the street to the left and she heard the others' footsteps racing behind her. She came to an intersection. "Which way?" she shouted.

"Left!"

She turned. They kept running, making three more quick turns and then she found herself in a park. Someone grabbed her arm and pulled her down behind a row of bushes. She turned just in time to see Solomon and Martin follow her and drop into crouched positions. She blinked at them. This entire time she had assumed it was Martin's hand on her, guiding her.

"Martin?"

He shook his head.

She turned and saw a ghost.

As Cindy screamed Jeremiah clamped a hand down over her mouth. "Ssh, it's me," he said, realizing belatedly that it was probably not the most reassuring thing he could have said to her at the moment, especially since he was still covered in makeup to make him appear dead.

"I'm not dead, I'm alive," he tried saying instead.

Her eyes were wide and her nostrils were flaring as she struggled to catch her breath and recover from the shock. Slowly he removed his hand from her mouth.

"You're not dead?" she whispered.

"No. But, I had to appear to be."

She hit him so fast that he never even saw her hand moving, just felt the explosive impact of it against his cheek.

"You deserved that," Martin said.

Martin would think so. He had never wanted to lie to Cindy in the first place.

"I will kill you," Cindy hissed.

"Actually not as easy to do as you'd think," Martin said. "If you'd like to try, though, I'd be happy to lend you my gun."

"Not helping," Jeremiah said, glaring at Martin.

The other man shrugged.

"What is going on?" Solomon asked, just as bewildered as Cindy.

"We had to flush out the traitor in your organization, the man who wanted Jeremiah dead from the start," Martin said. "So, we arranged a little dog and pony show for him."

"Why didn't you tell me?" Cindy demanded.

"I wanted to," Martin said quickly.

It was true. He had been planning on having Cindy in the loop from the start. He had reluctantly gone along with Jeremiah's plan. Jeremiah had told him that he didn't think Cindy could act the part well enough of the grieving wife if she knew the truth. Martin had seen through his lie and guessed the truth, though. Jeremiah had never planned to tell Cindy that he was alive.

He had made the decision to step out of her life in a way that would never leave her waiting or wondering but that would also spare them both the pain of the realization that she couldn't live with who he was and what he had done. It had seemed the right move, the smart one, for all involved. He hadn't planned for them to uncover the mole so quickly.

Martin should have put Cindy on a plane before they left the airport, but he hadn't. He'd have words with him later about that. Now Jeremiah's plan was ruined. He couldn't help but feel somewhere deep down that G-d had had a hand in that for some reason. Maybe Jeremiah was supposed to suffer rejection by Cindy for some reason.

Martin eased his head out around the hedge. "They're coming. We can't run forever."

"We can't be sure of picking them all off either," Solomon said.

Jeremiah nodded. "We split up. We meet up again in 12 hours at the Temple Mount. That should give both of you enough time to contact the people you trust."

"Let's just pray that nothing happens in those next 12 hours," Martin said.

"We won't live long enough to know one way or another unless we get out of here now," Solomon hissed.

"Time to go to ground. Gentlemen, see you in 12 hours," Martin said.

He burst out from behind the hedges and Jeremiah heard shouts as at least a few of their pursuers took off after him.

"Get ready to run," Jeremiah told Cindy.

"I don't know how much farther I can go," she said.

"I'll try to draw off those I can," Solomon said, nodding to Jeremiah.

The man leaped up and dashed in the opposite direction as Martin. Jeremiah could hear him drawing more searchers off.

"Stay low and with me," he said. He got into a crouch and starting moving deeper into the park, using bushes for cover. Cindy wasn't going to make it if things came down to a foot race so they had to be smarter instead of faster.

When he could hear her gasping for air he stopped behind a large fountain. She collapsed on the ground next to him. She was dressed as he'd last seen her, wearing someone else's clothes and her black scarf around her head. Jeremiah pulled off the blood-stained shirt with the bullet holes and the one beneath that. He used the undershirt to soak up some water from the fountain and quickly rub the makeup off his face.

"I thought you were dead," Cindy wheezed.

"I'm sorry you had to go through that," he said. "We needed everyone to believe."

"Haven't I done a good job acting this entire trip?"

"You have, and I'm sorry, but I worried that this would be too much and that the least little slip and you would be killed before I could help you."

It was a lie, but she didn't need to know that.

As soon as he got the makeup off, he looked around and spotted a gardener doing some work. The man was wearing his undershirt, sweating under the hot sun, while a plain looking white shirt rested on a bench a few yards away from him.

"Stay here, I will be right back," Jeremiah said.

It was a simple thing to grab the shirt. He did so and then made it back to Cindy. She was still looking haggard. She couldn't run much farther, but they had to go as far as they could as quickly as they could.

It was Friday and soon the sun would be setting.

He made a decision. One that cost him dearly. "Let's go," he said, reaching down for her hand.

Moments later they exited the park at a run. Jeremiah couldn't see anyone chasing them, but he couldn't stop until he knew they would not be found.

Cindy was still reeling from the revelation that Jeremiah was alive. She felt like she'd been put through an emotional wringer with so many wildly varying emotions slamming into her within seconds of each other.

Jeremiah was alive, but people were still trying to kill them.

Jeremiah had lied to her, but he was here with her.

"Where are we going?" Cindy gasped.

"Somewhere that I know you'll be safe," Jeremiah said. "But we will have to hurry."

They kept running, twisting through streets and alleys until Cindy thought she was going to collapse. At last they stopped in front of a house. Jeremiah turned to Cindy. "Whatever you do, do not answer any questions about who you are, where you're from, your last name, your profession, anything. Do you promise me that no matter what you will keep these things hidden for my sake?"

"Yes," she said, struggling to catch her breath.

"For what I'm about to do, I am sorry. For all of us."

As she pondered his words he turned and knocked on the door.

A few moments later it opened. A man stood there, a frown on his face. After a moment his eyes widened in surprise. He took a step backward, not as though he were inviting them in but as if he had seen a ghost and was moving away from the specter.

Jeremiah stepped into the house, pulling Cindy with him. The man closed the door and continued to stare at him.

Jeremiah's voice was tense as he said "Shalom, brother."

18

Cindy blinked and stared from one man to the other. They had the same chin, similar noses and cheekbones. The entire time they'd been over here he hadn't said one thing about his family. Yet here they were, standing in his brother's house.

"Shalom, Malachi," his brother whispered at last.

They just stood there, facing each other, for what seemed an eternity. Cindy wanted desperately to say something just to break the silence, but knew that she could not.

"Isaac, who is it?" a woman asked, appearing from out of a room in the back. She walked forward, got a good look at Jeremiah and let out a scream before collapsing onto the floor.

Jeremiah's hand tightened around hers, nearly crushing it. She squeezed to let him know that she was there for him, although he was so keyed up she wasn't sure he noticed the movement.

Other people quickly appeared, drawn by the sound of the scream. They were all speaking in a rush and Cindy couldn't understand them. Suddenly she felt Jeremiah jerk hard as if he had been electrocuted.

All sound stopped for a moment when Jeremiah turned and faced the new arrivals. On the floor the woman who had passed out groaned and started to sit up. Suddenly there was more agitated talking, shouts. The small crowd surged forward and an older woman laid hold of Jeremiah with tears in her eyes. She kissed his cheeks and then pulled him toward the back of the house.

Jeremiah kept his hand clamped around Cindy's and she got pulled forward along with him. Her head was spinning. These people must all be his relatives. The older woman was probably his mother. She didn't know how long it had been since any of them had seen him, but they acted as though they'd seen a ghost. She could relate.

They made it to the dining room where it was clear that they had been getting ready to eat dinner. Another chair was brought from somewhere and Jeremiah was pushed down into it. She stood next to him, still clutching his hand, not sure what she should do.

Suddenly all eyes turned on her with a mixture of curiosity and hostility and she took a deep breath. Clearly they were going to want to know who she was.

The hubbub gradually quieted as an older man began to speak. "Son, we had thought you were dead."

"It was safer for you to believe that, Father," Jeremiah said.

"How could you do that to Mother, to us?" the woman who had fainted demanded.

"Because it was necessary in order to do what I needed to do."

"He's talking in riddles," his mother said.

Another older man spoke up. "I told you who he worked for. You know why he had to leave. The question is, why is he back?"

"And who is she?" Isaac asked, indicating Cindy.

"We are here seeking shelter for a brief time in the home of my brother. I am sorry to have disturbed the whole family," Jeremiah said. He glanced at Cindy and he had a pained look in his eyes. Clearly this whole ordeal was costing him dearly. "This, this is my wife."

Cindy felt her heart stutter. Introducing her as such to spies and strangers was one thing, but he was lying to his parents and siblings about their relationship. He squeezed her hand even tighter.

"You married one of *them*?" the screaming woman asked in the ensuing silence.

"No, Ruth, I did not marry a Muslim." He took a deep breath. "I married a Christian."

More stunned silence greeted his proclamation. "Everyone, this is Cindy." He gave her a pained little smile. "It's okay to remove the scarf now."

Cindy reached up with her free hand and unwound the scarf from her head, shaking her hair slightly after it was free. She still wasn't used to how short it was. "Hello," she said.

"What about your children?" his mother asked.

Cindy took a deep breath. She knew that Judaism was traditionally passed through the mother's side.

"Our children, if G-d grants us any, will be raised by the most righteous woman I have ever known," Jeremiah said in a voice that was so intense it even took her aback.

The older man who was not his father came around the table. "I am Malachi's uncle, Jacob," he said to Cindy. "And I accept you as mishpacha, family. Shalom, Cindy." He reached out and embraced her then kissed each of her cheeks.

"Shalom, Uncle Jacob," Cindy said, trying not to stutter when she said 'uncle'.

He turned and headed for a seat at the table. "Shabbat is nearly upon us. Unless anyone else has something to say to Malachi's bride now I suggest we prepare," he said, sitting down.

Someone brought another chair and soon Cindy was seated next to Jeremiah. No one else had offered her a welcome, but at least they weren't asking her questions she wasn't allowed to answer.

Another younger woman who Cindy believed might be Isaac's wife lit the candles that were on the table. She waved her hands over them and then put her hands over her eyes while she recited something in Hebrew.

When she had finished she uncovered her eyes and looked at the candles for a moment.

"She is welcoming in and blessing the Shabbat," Jeremiah said quietly.

Ruth overheard, turned and glared at Cindy. "She doesn't even know how to keep the Shabbat?" she asked.

"Ruth, now is not the time," Jacob said gently.

Cindy desperately wanted to ask questions about the Sabbath and understand the meaning of everything, but she kept silent so as not to cause Jeremiah any more grief than he was already getting.

A couple of minutes passed while more food was piled on the table. The last thing placed down was a double loaf of bread that was then covered with a cloth. Finally a silver goblet was handed to Uncle Jacob who bowed his head over it and started to speak in Hebrew.

Very softly Jeremiah began translating for her benefit.

"And there was evening and there was morning, a sixth day. The heavens and the

192

earth were finished, the whole host of them.
And on the seventh day God completed his
work that he had done, and he rested on the
seventh day from all his work that he had
done. And God blessed the seventh day and
sanctified it, because in it he had rested from
all his work that God had created to do.
Blessed are you, Lord, our God, Sovereign of
the Universe, Who creates the fruit of the
vine."

"Amen," everyone said.

"Blessed are You, Lord, our God, King of the
Universe, Who sanctifies us with His
commandments, and has been pleased with us,
You have lovingly and willingly given us
Your holy Shabbat as an inheritance, in
memory of creation because it is the first day
of our holy assemblies, in memory of the
exodus from Egypt because You have chosen
us and made us holy from all peoples, and
have willingly and lovingly given us Your
holy Shabbat for an inheritance.
Blessed are You, who sanctifies Shabbat."

"Amen," they said again and Cindy was able to get the
word out as well.

Uncle Jacob drank from the cup and then passed it to
Jeremiah's father who drank and passed it along. When it
came to Jeremiah he drank and then gave it to her with a
slight nod. She hesitantly took a sip. It was wine and she

struggled not to wrinkle her nose at the taste. She passed it to Isaac who took it without a word.

Once everyone had taken a sip of the wine, Jacob pulled a basin toward him. "Now we wash our hands," Jeremiah told her.

There was a cup of water in front of every person. Jacob picked up his, then held his hands over the empty bowl and poured the water first over one hand then the other. He recited something in Hebrew before drying his hands and passing the bowl.

Each person did as he had. Cindy glanced at Jeremiah. When it was his turn he said the blessing in English. "Blessed are You, Lord, our God, King of the Universe who has sanctified us with His commandments and commanded us concerning washing of hands."

It was Cindy's turn. She poured water over one hand then the other. "Blessed are You, our God, King of the Universe who has sanctified us and commanded us concerning washing of hands." She knew she'd left some words out, but it was the best she could do under the circumstances. Jeremiah gave her a smile which made her feel better.

Once they had all washed their hands Jacob uncovered the bread, spoke a short blessing over it, and then broke it into pieces and passed it around so that each had some. Cindy sat with her piece of bread in her hands. She was starving. Being close to all the food when she'd gone for so long without eating was starting to make her a little crazy. She was actually reminded of the Passover dinner at Marie's house when she and Jeremiah were first getting to know each other. Suddenly the record-breakingly short prayers her father had always said over holiday meals seemed like a really good idea.

"What now?" she whispered.

"Now, my love, we eat."

"Oh thank heavens," she breathed.

Jeremiah couldn't have been more proud of Cindy. She was holding up well under the pressure and the foreignness of it all. It had cost him dearly to tell his family that they were married, perpetuating the lie he had told to Solomon. It had to be done, though.

He had not expected the rest of the family to be at his brother's home that night. He had hoped it would just be Isaac and his wife, Lily, at home. The presence of his parents, uncle, sister and brother-in-law made things harder and more complicated. It was hard to look at them all. It had been so many years since he had laid eyes on them that when he did he ached inside.

That was the cost of his job and his forced retirement, though. His uncle understood. While he was working for the Mossad he'd had a colleague who would check up on them once in a while, make sure everyone was okay. He hadn't been there when either of his siblings had gotten married, but a friend had given him all the details. In exchange he had provided information to that friend about his family which he was also staying away from to protect.

When Jeremiah had retired he'd had to give up even that. He couldn't let his old colleague know where he was or who he was pretending to be so even information about his family had stopped coming to him.

"How long have you been married?" Isaac asked.

"A little less than two weeks," Jeremiah said. That fit with the time frame he'd told Solomon.

"And how did you meet?" Lily asked Cindy.

Cindy turned and looked at Jeremiah. He smiled at her. "Generalities are fine."

Cindy nodded then turned to Lily. "I was going into work early in the morning. I was there before anyone else and in the dark I literally tripped over a dead body. I fell and when I realized what I'd tripped over I started screaming. J- Malachi was close by and heard my screams and came to my rescue."

Lily's eyes were wide. "That must have been terrible for you."

"It was, but had it not been for that I might never have met Malachi."

"Was the dead man your doing?" his father asked him bluntly.

"No, that one was not," Jeremiah said with dark significance.

"How could you ask such a thing?" his mother said.

"You know what he does for a living. Or, at least, what we think he does for a living."

Uncle Jacob spoke up. "Please, it is the Shabbat, we should not be discussing business."

"Very true," Lily said, clearly struggling to be a good hostess despite everything. "So, was it love at first sight?"

"It was for me. She took some convincing," Jeremiah said, putting his arm around Cindy's shoulders and squeezing them.

"At least, that's what I let him think," Cindy said with a smile.

Lily laughed. "I like her," she said spontaneously.

Cindy's grin widened.

"How do you reconcile the fact that you believe in two different religions?" Ruth asked, her tone openly hostile.

Jeremiah started to speak, but Cindy cut him off. "It pains me, deeply, that Jeremiah doesn't share all of my beliefs. I'm a Protestant. Judaism is like a grandparent religion to mine. Everything I learn about your religion and culture helps deepen my understanding of the traditions and teachings of mine. It's been very eye-opening and has led me to deeper faith. I believe there is so much beauty in your traditions that has been lost. I plan on finding ways to reincorporate those traditions, the meanings of things into my own religion and worship. And, I pray every day, that someday, somehow Jeremiah will begin to incorporate some of my beliefs into his as well."

"But you married him anyway, without him having done so?" Ruth asked, sounding suspicious.

Cindy straightened. "I'd never met a man I could love before I met him. He's everything I never knew I wanted. I'm alive with him. I'm my best with him. He has taken a shy, terrified girl and turned me into a strong woman. In the end, I couldn't deny my heart. And I continue to live in hope."

Jeremiah refused to tear up in front of his family, but at that moment he wanted to. There were so many emotions swirling around in him and there was so much longing and confusion. Cindy had become a good actress, but was she really that good? Was she just making it all up or did she really feel that way about him and the religious differences they had?

There was silence around the table in the wake of Cindy's speech. Finally his father cleared his throat. "Why have you come here today? It couldn't have been because you cared that we meet your bride or you would have shown up before the wedding."

"I did not want to cause so much distress. I came here today because I was desperate. We needed a place to hide and I knew no one would look for us here. As soon as it is safe, we will be on our way. It has never been my intention to put any of you in danger which is why I've stayed away. Today I had no choice. The work I am doing right now is important. It will save us all, but not if I get killed before I can finish it. But then, as Uncle Jacob so wisely pointed out, it is Shabbat and we should not be discussing work."

"Twice now you have said that you have stayed away to protect us," his mother said. "Yet you have taken a wife. Do you not care to protect her?"

"I have worried about that since the moment I met her. I wanted to free her to live a life of safety without me, but G-d wouldn't let me." Cindy needn't ever know how many times he'd tried to leave including this latest. He continued, his voice catching, "My life has been one of uncertainty for so long. He showed me that it doesn't matter where I am or what I'm doing, because she is the only home I need."

Tears were sparkling in Cindy's eyes as she looked up at him and her lips were trembling. He reached out and hugged her as best he could. As he pulled away he made a decision.

Coming here had been a bad idea. It was breaking him down emotionally. It wasn't a response to seeing his family for the first time in years, but rather having to talk about his relationship with Cindy. Everything he had just said was true, but it didn't help him to maintain his focus on the task at hand.

He stood, hardening himself as he did so. "We should go."

Cindy quickly shoved another bite of food in her mouth. He knew she was hungry, but it was time. They had gained a few precious minutes hiding here, and now they would go. She stood up and he put his hand on her shoulder, intent on steering her toward the door.

"Please, don't," Lily pleaded, standing as well.

Jeremiah met his uncle's eyes. Jacob gave him a small nod. He understood and did not condemn him. His parents and Ruth were glaring at him. Isaac and Ruth's husband both kept their eyes down, refusing to look at him.

Jeremiah knew that this was likely the last time he'd see anyone at that table again. He had longed for so many years to be with them, but he realized now that it wasn't possible. There was too much he could never tell them and only two who would be willing to listen even if they could.

It had been wrong to come here. He never would have if he'd known his parents and Ruth were there. He knew that seeing him had been a shock, one that given time they might have been able to overcome. But there was no future path in which he could come back to them alive. They deserved to know that so they would not be left waiting and wondering. That was Cindy's greatest fear. That was why she was here with him instead of somewhere safer. He could at least spare his family that misery.

He stood tall. He took hold of his shirt on the left side over his heart. "Father." He ripped the shirt, symbolizing that the relationship was ended as if by death.

"No!" Lily wailed.

"Mother," he said, tearing the shirt again.

"How dare you?" Ruth hissed at him.

He grabbed the shirt on the right side and tore it as he said, "Ruth." He tore it again as he named her husband.

Lily was sobbing. His brother, Isaac, still refused to look up. Uncle Jacob met his gaze with compassion and understanding. Jeremiah could not rend his garment for him. He was about to rend it for Isaac when Lily caught hold of Cindy's hands.

"You are my sister-in-law. You are my family," she said, kissing Cindy's cheeks. "Isaac. Do something; it's your *brother*. He came to us in need and we must not let him go this way."

Isaac rose slowly from his chair. He kept his eyes on the ground, but he addressed Jeremiah. "Do not do this thing, Malachi."

"For your wife's sake, I will not," Jeremiah said.

He turned and moved toward the front of the house. Cindy walked with him, quiet, pale, but with her head held high. Just before they reached the door, Uncle Jacob put a hand on each of them. Jeremiah turned. The pain he should be feeling he'd managed to suppress into a little ball and push to the back of his mind. Finality could provide its own kind of relief if you let it.

"This was not about you," Jacob told Cindy gravely. "You must not let yourself be troubled by it. I wish you and my nephew a lifetime of joy and blessings."

"Thank you, Uncle," she murmured before kissing his cheeks.

"It isn't safe out there. It's Shabbat, noone will be on the streets except for you and those looking for you."

"I know."

"And the clothing we rend in mourning is not to be worn on Shabbat, so you will be even more noticeable."

200

Jeremiah nodded. It was the price he was willing to pay.

His uncle swiftly took off his own shirt. "Here, please," he said.

Jeremiah switched shirts. "Thank you."

"It is nothing."

"You can find me?" Jeremiah asked him.

"If I need to then I believe I can. But I don't intend to need to."

"Be well," Jeremiah told him.

The older man nodded sagely.

Jeremiah opened the door and together he and Cindy walked out of his brother's house. And as he breathed in the air outside he realized just how true what he'd said inside was. Cindy was the only home he had. The only one he needed.

19

As they hurried down the street Cindy was still reeling from shock. She couldn't even begin to imagine how Jeremiah must be feeling. They moved into a darkened alley and then he stopped and turned to face her.

"I am sorry," he said.

"You already apologized before we went into the house."

"I did not realize that my parents would be there. Had I known I never would have taken you into that situation."

"It's okay," she said, trying to smile reassuringly. "My family's dinners can be really awkward, too."

He smiled for just a moment, but at least it was something. Then the cold, hard mask slipped back into place again. "Uncle was right. We need to get off the streets."

"I'm ready for this day to end," Cindy muttered.

Of all things they ended up in a small, American cafe, one of the few places in town that was not closed for Shabbat.

"No one will think of looking for us in the open," Jeremiah said.

Cindy tore into a cheeseburger with gusto and as soon as she had finished she ordered a second one. Jeremiah was eating as well, but much more slowly and he kept stopping frequently to stare at her. If she hadn't been so famished it would have been distracting. After she finished the second burger she took a long sip of Coca Cola. Nothing had ever tasted sweeter.

She took a deep breath and looked at him. "You put me through hell," she said bluntly. She wasn't overly fond of using that word, but it certainly fit.

"I'm sorry," he said, dropping his eyes to the table.

He was hiding something from her. She could feel it. She just couldn't figure out what it was.

"You certainly trusted Martin to play his role well," she said with a slight dusting of sarcasm.

It was amazing how much more rational she felt on a full stomach. If only she could find some comfortable clothes then life would be good. Well, not good, but leaps and bounds beyond what it had been.

"It's his job to lie to people," Jeremiah said distractedly.

There was a lot of tension between them. She didn't know how much of it had to do with everything that had happened at his parents'. She had said things and so had he. Hers had been true and she found herself wondering about the things he had said about them, their relationship. Then there was the fact that she really wanted to slap him again for all the grief he had caused her. Yet, in the back of her mind a little voice kept urging to not waste the gift that she had been given: a second chance to tell him how she felt about him.

"You said some very nice things back there."

"They were true," he said, refusing to look at her.

She could feel her heart begin to beat a little faster. "Thank you."

He still refused to look at her and she realized it might not be the ideal time to have a heart-to-heart.

"What's going to happen in the morning when we meet up with the others?" she asked.

"Hopefully one of them will have come up with a plan."

"Why aren't we working on a plan?" she asked.

"Because we have limited resources and an overwhelming need to stay alive."

She thrummed her fingers on the table. He was being so closed off it was both annoying and frightening. She glanced outside. There was a drugstore open on the other side of the street.

"Do you think that store would have sweats, jeans, or something other than what I'm wearing?" she asked.

He looked up at her with a frown. "Are you still wearing your other clothes under those?"

"Yes, and I'm not sure which is more uncomfortable. Maybe I can just go take a look."

He stood hastily. "I will look. You stay here."

She watched him cross the street and enter the store. She kept her eyes glued to the door. She had a fear deep down that he'd somehow manage to sneak off, thinking it was safer to leave her in the restaurant.

A couple of minutes later he reemerged with a bag. She relaxed when he finally walked back into the restaurant. He sat down and handed her the bag.

"It's the best I could do. It's still a dress, but it should at least be more comfortable."

She nodded and thought with longing of her suitcase full of clothes at the hotel. When this was over would she see any of those things again? There was a restroom in the restaurant and she got up.

"If you're not sitting right there when I get back, I'll kill you," she said.

He nodded absently.

She headed to the restroom to change clothes. The dress he'd bought was a very soft cotton one that was grey in color. She kept her slip that she'd been wearing under the other clothes but dumped the rest of them in the trash. She scrubbed her face in the sink. She was almost starting to feel human again, although she really could go for a shower. Hopefully when this was over she could find a nice hot one and just stay in it for a day. Feeling better she headed back to their table.

Jeremiah looked up as Cindy sat back down across from him. She looked beautiful and how she managed to do that despite everything he didn't know. He started to tell her, but then snapped his mouth shut. It seemed like everything that happened, every word that was spoken, just made the inevitable harder on both of them.

They finally left the diner and were able to take a taxi for a short distance. The cab driver was openly curious about them and eventually Jeremiah had him drop them off in front of a hotel. As soon as he was out of sight they took their time making it the rest of the way to the Temple Mount. It was a long walk and they had to stick mostly to shadows. Cindy's steps were dragging by the time they got close.

"How do you know we'll catch the terrorists here today?" she asked.

"They're running out of time on their original time table. Plus, they will have accelerated things knowing that we know at least some of their identities."

"They may still think you're dead," she said.

"Perhaps, perhaps not."

He stopped. "We're here," he said.

"Where?"

"The Western Wall."

"You mean, the Wailing Wall?" Cindy asked, a note of awe in her voice.

"Yes, it is one of the four walls that encompasses and supports the Temple Mount," Jeremiah said. "Many believe that it is the sole remaining remnant of the Temple, part of the outer courtyard. It is as close as Jews can come to the site of the Temple and pray since it is forbidden by law for any but Muslims to pray inside the walls. Many believe that when the Holy of Holies was destroyed with the Temple that G-d sent his spirit to reside here. People come to weep, pray. Mystics come to have visions of G-d. Every year on Tisha B'Av tens of thousands gather to commemorate the destruction of the Temple."

"Isn't that the date which one of the conspirators was hoping to set off the destruction of the Dome of the Rock?"

"Yes. Doing so would destroy one of the Muslim's most sacred sites, clearing the way for the rebuilding of the Temple, but it would also kill almost one hundred thousand Jews if the blast was large enough. We are both lucky and unlucky that they will not wait the extra few days to strike."

"It is here that people write prayers and put them in the wall?" Cindy asked.

"Yes, if you wish to, please do."

"I have nothing to write with."

"Perhaps one of our friends can help," Jeremiah said as he saw the figure of a man begin to walk toward them.

A moment later Martin was standing with them. "I figured this was where you meant to meet," he said.

Jeremiah nodded.

"Do you have paper and a pen?" Cindy asked.

He nodded and pulled them out of his coat pocket. Jeremiah watched as she scribbled a note. He wondered what she was praying for.

"I would think it's been more than thirty days, Rabbi, since you've seen the Wall. Aren't you required to rend your clothes in grief?"

"Not on the Shabbat," Jeremiah said evenly.

"Forgive me, how could I have forgotten?"

"Yes, and none of us is covering our heads and I'm sure each of us is carrying an electronic item. We are all desecrating the place," Jeremiah said.

"But as I remember, all Sabbath rules may be broken to save lives."

"You are correct," Jeremiah acknowledged.

Cindy folded up her piece of paper and stuffed it in a crack of the Wall. She returned the pen and pad of paper to Martin just as Solomon appeared out of the darkness.

"I've stationed men I can trust from the Israeli military at the Mugrabi Gate. They will allow only us to pass that way," Solomon said without preamble. "What other men I have that I can trust I have patrolling the walls."

"That's fine unless our enemies are already inside," Martin said drily. "I have ten men already inside the walls. Two are inside the Dome of the Rock itself, hiding, waiting."

"Which is fine unless our enemies are outside the walls," Solomon said.

Cindy fought down the urge to tell them to play nice with each other.

"I will remain outside, see if I can find anything suspicious," Solomon said.

"I'll be going in to be with my men."

"Aren't there three structures on the Temple Mound?" Cindy asked.

"Yes," Jeremiah responded. "There is the al-Aqsa Mosque, the shrine that is the Dome of the Rock, and also a free-standing dome that is used as a prayer house called the Dome of the Chain.

"Then how do we know they're going after the Dome of the Rock and not one of the other two?"

"Because the Dome of the Rock is the one sitting exactly where the Temple is supposed to be rebuilt," Solomon said. "It would be the biggest target, the most obvious call to war for all sides."

"We will go inside as well," Jeremiah said. "We need all the eyes we can get if the bomb or bombs have already been placed. And, if they haven't, we're going to need all the fighters we have to keep them from being installed."

"Okay, lead the way so you can tell your men we're good to pass," Martin said to Solomon.

"Remember, if you see anyone, we need to take at least one of them alive for questioning. We need to make sure we take down this entire cell," Solomon said.

Something was bothering Cindy as she walked with Jeremiah toward the Dome of the Rock after having been waved through the gate by Solomon's men. Everything that people said about blowing up the Dome of the Rock made sense. Israeli zealots looking to rebuild the Temple could certainly be tempted to blow up the shrine. It did also make a certain amount of sense that Arabs wanting to have an excuse to destroy Israel would target it. However, she had a hard time believing that Muslims would blow up a site that was so sacred even for a chance to strike at their enemy. It was possible that whoever was behind this plot was only recruiting Arabs who weren't overly religious, but it still bothered her.

Even as her mind was working overtime she couldn't help but be awed by the massive structures that were looming up out of the ground. It was not yet daylight but she could still see the gold colored dome against the early morning sky. Once inside Martin switched on a flashlight and swept it over millions of brilliantly colored tiles. Arch topped columns reached for the heavens.

Cindy could make out at least half a dozen other flashlights casting back and forth in the darkness. One of them shone right in her eyes as its bearer approached.

"Found anything yet?" Martin asked.

"Nothing," the man behind the light answered.

"Okay, leave half the men inside and put the other half outside. Kill the flashlights, we don't want to telegraph our presence if we don't need to." Martin sighed. "And now we wait."

Jeremiah grabbed Cindy's hand and pulled her over to one wall where they slowly sat down. As soon as she was seated Cindy felt her eyes starting to shut.

"It's been a long time since you slept, go ahead," Jeremiah urged.

She shook her head trying to clear it. "No, I can't."

"Why not? It could be hours before anyone shows, if they even make it past the guards outside."

"Something's wrong, I can feel it," Cindy told him.

"What?"

"I don't know." She let out a frustrated sigh. "So, if this is a shrine, what's it to?"

He pointed toward the middle of the floor, beneath the dome. "The Foundation Stone."

"What's that?" she asked.

"According to many Jewish scholars it is the stone on which Abraham attempted to sacrifice Isaac. It is also thought to be either the stone that sat beneath the Ark of the Covenant or the stone that sat beneath the altar in the Temple. Its resting place being the location of the Holy of Holies is the most agreed upon. Jews from all over the world pray in the direction of the Foundation Stone."

"I did not know that," she said.

"Muslims used to pray facing the Foundation Stone as well. Only they believed that it was Ishmael that Abraham almost sacrificed instead of Isaac. Mohammed eventually claimed to have a revelation which deemed that Muslims should start praying facing Mecca instead. They still have many legends associated with this place, though. Directly beneath the rock is a cave that is called the Well of Souls. It is significant in both Jewish and Muslim tradition."

Cindy's growing feeling of unease exploded within her, and it was strong enough to catapult her to her feet.

"What's wrong?" Jeremiah asked sharply.

"This is. All of it."

"You said that before; tell me what it is you're feeling," Jeremiah said, rising to stand next to her.

"I had a hard time believing that Arabs would purposely blow up this shrine even if it meant they would have a chance to wipe out Israel for good. Now, I know that this is the wrong place. Even if I could believe that, I refuse to believe that zealous Israelis would blow up this structure. They wouldn't want to risk harming the Foundation Stone or the cave below it. No, they want to destroy this place and rebuild the Temple, but they'll tear down the shrine with bulldozers and hammers. They won't blow a crater in the Mount."

"I understand your logic, but what else could it be?" he asked.

"This entire site is sacred. Now, I could see the Israelis blowing up the mosque, but I still have a problem seeing the Arabs going along with that. If this was just one group of people we could make sense of it, but these are groups who have very opposite views who can both agree on the destruction of one thing that will result in both the rebuilding of the Temple and all out war between Israel and her neighbors."

"I think I know where you're heading with this," he said.

She nodded. "I don't think they ever meant to blow up this building. I think they're going to blow up the Dome of the Chain."

"Martin!" Jeremiah shouted, running for the entrance. Cindy scrambled to keep up with him.

Moments later the other man was beside them. "What?"

"Cindy thinks this isn't their target. She thinks they're going to blow up the Dome of the Chain instead."

"What? But why?"

"We'll explain later," Jeremiah said.

They raced outside and across the ground toward the much smaller structure. As they neared it Jeremiah slowed. Martin turned on his flashlight, sweeping it over the building which had no exterior wall.

"The structure is named for a legend regarding King Solomon. According to Muslim tradition it's also the place where Judgment Day will occur and the sinful shall be parted from the righteous."

Martin stepped inside, lifting his flashlight up into the dome. Suddenly he froze.

Jeremiah walked forward and Cindy grabbed his hand tight and walked with him. There, partway up the one arch, was something that had to be a bomb.

She had been right. Martin turned to look at her with a surprised expression on his face.

"I told you that you needed me," she said.

"Jackson, Ellis, to me!" he shouted.

Jeremiah pulled her away from it as two of Martin's men came running up.

"We have to get that disarmed now!" Martin snapped as he painted the bomb with his flashlight. "Get on it, I'll check to see if there are any more on the structure. Move, move, move!"

Jeremiah pulled Cindy further away. Moments later more of his men were running from the larger dome to join him at the smaller one.

"Start looking for secondary devices," she heard Martin barking.

"We found it," she said. "Do you think they can disarm it?"

"Hopefully," Jeremiah said, pulling her farther back from the dome and the men scrambling around it. "But right now we've got a bigger problem."

"What's that?" Cindy asked, turning to look at him.

"They're here," he whispered.

20

Men were pouring out of the mosque, guns and knives held high.

Jeremiah shouted at the top of his lungs to get the attention of the C.I.A. agents and hopefully Solomon's men outside the wall. He grabbed the gun from his waistband, wishing he'd picked up some more ammunition, and dropped the first four men who reached him.

"Run for the Rock!" Jeremiah shouted to Cindy.

She turned and sprinted for the large dome. He felt a bullet whiz past his head as he dropped to the ground to grab a gun off one of the dead men. He managed to grab a knife as well.

He scrambled to his feet, keeping low and weaving to make a difficult target, especially in the dark. He heard a scream and he turned to see a woman grabbing at Cindy. Cindy kicked her in the knee and spun out of her grasp.

Jeremiah ran over. The woman who'd grabbed Cindy had flaming red hair. She was also holding the torn remnants of Cindy's dress. Jeremiah dropped her with a single shot and chased after Cindy into the Dome of the Rock.

Cindy was standing under the dome in her slip. All the agents who had been inside were now outside, most of them closer to the other dome. Some of them were fighting, others were trying to disarm the bomb. They couldn't do that if they were dead.

"Hide," Jeremiah hissed before he headed back outside. He had to buy those agents as much time as he could.

He began firing, dropping more of the enemy. There were so many more of them than he had anticipated. Out of the corner of his eye he saw at least four of the American agents go down.

He shot another man who wasn't carrying a gun, but instead had something tucked under his arm. As he tumbled to the ground it fell, too. Jeremiah's stomach sank when he saw that it was a black box. Another bomb.

He sprinted forward and snatched it up. It hadn't been armed yet. One of the men on the field of battle turned and saw him with the bomb. "Get him!" he screamed to his compatriots, pointing at Jeremiah.

Suddenly a wave of attackers was coming his way. An American agent got to him first. "We disarmed it!" he shouted.

"Great," Jeremiah growled. "Get this one out of here."

He handed it off to the other man who just kept running. Jeremiah pantomimed still holding the box to give the other man time to get away with it. It worked. The wave of men kept coming toward him.

Jeremiah retreated into the building. Cindy was partway down the series of marble steps that led into the Well of Souls.

"They're coming!" he shouted to her.

He dropped to the floor and a hail of bullets went over his head. He fired off three rapid rounds and then he was out from the gun he'd taken off the dead man. He managed to roll behind one of the pillars. He had felled two of his enemies. That left six more. They had guns. He just had a knife.

Then it happened, the clicking of empty magazines. With a swift prayer he leaped from his hiding place and waded into his attackers, slashing with the knife. He caught one man across the throat and he fell in a spray of blood. Jeremiah turned and plunged the blade into another one's chest, yanking it out. He turned and felt fire trace its way across his ribs.

He spun to find a man facing him with a knife as his comrades were frantically trying to reload. With three quick strikes the man was dead and his knife belonged to Jeremiah.

Then a gun came up and he threw himself behind another pillar. They advanced and he managed to make it to the next pillar, drawing them farther into the structure. Then came the clicking as they were again out of bullets. He started to step out from behind the pillar but a shot rang out and just grazed his shoulder. They were getting smart. They had him pinned and they weren't all changing their clips at once.

Outside the sound of firing had died down. Jeremiah wondered how many were left on either side.

Cindy was practically eye level to the ground. None of Jeremiah's attackers had seen her crouched on the stairs. Suddenly he leaped out from behind a pillar and threw a knife which lodged in one man's chest. He threw the second knife and another man fell. The last man standing was still trying to reload his gun. He tossed it to the side and grabbed for one of the knives. Jeremiah pulled the other one out of the body it was lodged in. The two men fought, slipping over the ground and each nearly falling half a dozen times. Cindy wanted to scream, but she dared not. All had gone quiet outside. She wondered if everyone was dead.

The other man got in two good swings, tearing Jeremiah's shirt and drawing blood. She glanced around, looking for a gun she could get to. There was nothing near her. She'd have to run past them to try to get one and she couldn't risk distracting Jeremiah.

The other man jumped forward and swung. Jeremiah stepped, turned into him and snatched the knife out of his hand before plunging both knives into the man's chest and then pulling them out as he fell.

Then all was silent. Slowly Cindy crept up the stairs until she was crouched on the floor of the building.

He turned to look at her and his gaze burned right through her. He was like some terrible, avenging angel.

Angel of Death.

She understood now why they called him that. She looked around. They were surrounded by bodies. Blood was splattered everywhere. She turned back to Jeremiah and looked at the knives he clenched in each fist.

"This is who I am," he said fiercely. He raised the knives in the air and then let them fall to the ground on either side of him.

"I know," she sobbed. She rose to her feet and walked slowly toward him. "I've always known. Ever since that first week. You killed that man, that monster, to save me. You did it without thinking, without hesitating. You were so fast. No one else saw, but I did. And I knew exactly what you were."

She stopped mere inches from him. She put her hand on his blood-streaked chest, over his heart. "I've always known who you were in here."

He stared down at her, eyes burning through her. She reached up and grabbed his face in her hands and pulled it down. Her heart was pounding as she kissed his lips. It was just a peck, just a moment, but she had to do it before she lost her nerve. She let go of him and stepped back.

He stared into her eyes. "This is who I am, you understand? I tried to hide it. I'm sorry."

"I'm not," she said.

He bent down, keeping his eyes locked on hers. His were searching, questioning. She smiled, and a moment later he kissed her. The kiss was gentle, almost hesitating. She kissed him back.

It was as though a dam broke inside him and he crushed her to him, kissing her harder, deeper. She closed her eyes and wrapped her arms around his neck, giving herself over to what felt like a lifetime of longing.

He sank to his knees and she went with him. He kept holding her and he buried his face in her shoulder. "Don't leave me," he sobbed.

"Never," she breathed, kissing the crown of his head and running her hands through his hair.

He looked up at her, his face contorted in anguish. "You know everything," he said.

"I do."

"I never let myself kiss you, all the times I wanted to, because you didn't know everything."

"Now I know."

"And you're not running away?"

"No."

"Deep down this is who I am, not Jeremiah, but this."

"I don't care what name you use or what you do." She hesitated, about to admit something to him that she hadn't dreamed she would. "I love you because of who you are, not despite it."

He kissed her again, breathing words against her lips that she couldn't understand. Even though he was speaking in Hebrew her heart knew what he was saying. He pulled away and looked in her eyes. He put his hands behind her head, holding it, cradling it.

"I've given you every chance to leave me," he whispered.

"I know. I won't leave you."

"Then God have mercy on you because I can't hold myself back anymore."

Suddenly he was kissing her again, harder, faster until she couldn't catch her breath. "I love you," he said between kisses, his voice thick with emotion. "I am yours - mind, heart, and body. Whatever you want from me I give it to you."

She shuddered, her very soul longing for him. "I want you..." she whispered, straining to get the words out.

"I am yours," he said, his voice shaking. He pulled her tighter against him and her back arched as she responded to him.

"I want you to stop lying about being my husband," she managed to say.

He pulled back and stared at her with a stricken look even as his hands stroked her cheeks. He nodded slowly. "Why?" he whispered and she could hear pain in his voice. He didn't understand her.

"Because I want you to be my husband, and I want to be your wife. And then," she said, letting her hands drift slowly across his stomach, "I'll take everything I want."

"We both will," he said, voice ragged.

They continued to stare at each other for a moment and then he stood, pulling her up with him. Her legs felt a little shaky and as if sensing that, he put his arm around her and held her up.

"Time to go back home," he said. They started walking and her legs began to feel a bit stronger. "I can't lie to you. It's not going to be easy to transition back into that life after everything that's happened here."

"Nothing's ever easy for us. Why should this be any different?"

They made it outside just as Solomon ran up to him. "The bombs are defused and away from here. We've got twenty dead terrorists out here."

"There's eight inside," Jeremiah said.

Solomon's eyes nearly bulged out of his head. "I told you, we needed one of them alive for questioning."

Jeremiah just stared at him for a long moment and then shook his head. "It's been a while, so I guess maybe you've forgotten. I don't leave survivors."

21

Cindy couldn't believe that they were finally on a plane headed home. She didn't actually breathe easy until the plane had taken off and was in the air. Then she allowed herself to relax in her seat.

Martin had survived the Battle of Temple Mount as they had all started to call it, but he had lost five of his men in the fighting. All twenty-eight of the terrorists who had been present that morning had been killed, much to Solomon's chagrin. Among them were six current and former Mossad agents, ten Arabs, and a dozen Russians. Martin had sworn that the one was KGB although he couldn't prove that the red-haired woman still worked for that agency.

That was what had everyone the most frustrated. The evidence seemed to point to her and the others having actively recruited the others, but no one could prove that the Russian government had a hand in it, even though they were one of the few countries who would stand to profit mightily from a war in the Middle East.

With no one alive to question they couldn't even be sure they had captured all the active conspirators. She did know that Khalid was among the dead as was Solomon's driver. So, she let herself hope that they had stopped the threat once and for all.

Officially the whole incident was being swept under the rug with drunken teenagers being blamed for the shots that so many people had reported hearing. The Dome of the

Rock was officially closed for cleaning which meant patching bullet holes and scrubbing blood stains. All-in-all the damage done to the structures had been surprisingly minimal in contrast to that done to people.

After three days of what they called debriefing, Jeremiah and Cindy had finally been told they were free to return home. She had secretly worried that after he had helped save the world the Mossad would decide they needed Jeremiah to remain an active member, but they had let him go in the end.

They had been reunited with their luggage, which had been a relief, and she had taken at least six long, hot showers in the last three days. Everything should be returning to normal soon.

Well, the new normal, whatever that was going to look like. She knew one thing for sure, she was coming home a changed person and she knew that Jeremiah might have some surface wounds but the real injuries were to his spirit. She would help him heal. She could be patient. For a while.

They hadn't talked about it, but every night since as she went to sleep she had relived the kisses they'd shared and the things that they had said to each other.

"I can't wait to get home," she said.

"Yeah. When I called Mark he said they had a surprise for us. He said he'd pick us up at the airport, too."

"That will be good. I wonder what the surprise is?"

Jeremiah shrugged. "He didn't say."

Cindy glanced down at his hands and noticed with a start that he had not yet taken the platinum ring off his left hand.

"You're still wearing the wedding ring," Cindy said softly.

"Yes."

"Why?"

Jeremiah turned and looked her in the eyes. "As a reminder to myself of what I'm working toward. It wasn't easy for me to shed the darkness the first time. This time it's going to be even harder I fear. This is to remind me that I'm trying to be a man who is worthy of your affection."

He couldn't bring himself to say the word "love". He was still reeling from everything that had been said between them, the feeling of her lips against his.

"You don't have to work on being that," she said. "You already are."

He didn't say anything. Extreme circumstances could cause a person to make crazy promises that the real world would never let them keep. He didn't doubt that Cindy cared for him. He would never doubt that again. But he would not hold her to anything she had said until life had calmed down and he was a semblance of the man she had known for so long. That would give her time to rethink if necessary.

"What is Marie going to say?"

He didn't care one iota what his secretary would say. That was part of the problem. The killer in him didn't fit well into civilized society. He needed to cultivate the other part of his personality, the rabbi who cared about people and their thoughts and feelings. It was just going to take time to make that switch. He had done it before. He could do it again.

And he knew she would help him.

He reached out and took her hand and squeezed it in his. "Have I told you today how beautiful you are?"

She shook her head.

"Then I'm an idiot and clearly a blind and mute one at that."

She smiled and it was the most beautiful thing in the world to him.

He cupped her cheek with his hand. "You are the most radiant creature that walks the earth."

He started to bend down. He wanted to kiss her. He hesitated, though.

"Don't be that way," she said. She twisted her fingers in his hair and pulled his face down to hers. She kissed him, not a gentle kiss, but a kiss that held a promise of days to come for them. He closed his eyes and held on to that promise, happy to kiss her until those days were their present and not their future.

Mark was waiting at baggage claim, anxious to see Cindy and Jeremiah safe and in one piece. Jeremiah hadn't been able to explain anything to him over the phone, so he was hoping to get some answers as well.

At last he saw them and he waved. Cindy ran forward and threw her arms around him joyously. "I'm so happy to see you!" she said. Usually she was a little more reserved and it took him by surprise, but he hugged her back. Her hair was cut super short and he wondered what had happened to it. Before he could say anything she stepped away and he turned to Jeremiah.

Mark had looked coldblooded killers in the eye and seen more warmth than he saw in Jeremiah's eyes now.

The man's face was a smooth, cold mask. Mark had known for a long time that Jeremiah hid things from him and that he had a tremendous poker face, but even when they didn't know each other, he'd never looked this cold and unattached.

It shook him. He forced himself to take a deep breath. "Right. Well, let's get your luggage and get out of here," he said.

Ten minutes later they were all in the car and headed back to Pine Springs.

"I'm sorry Traci isn't here," Cindy said, clearly disappointed.

"Oh, you'll see her when we get where we're going," Mark assured her. "Now, tell me what happened."

They took the rest of the drive to fill him in and by the end he was completely floored. There were several things they were clearly leaving out, but he at least got the basics.

"Thank you, Mark," Cindy said. "Your information helped save the world."

He felt suddenly warm inside. "Well, it's not every day you get to help do that," he said.

"Where are we going?" Jeremiah asked as they neared the hospital.

"Oh, to see Traci and meet a couple of new friends. You see, while you two were busy stopping World War III we were having some excitement of our own back here."

He felt himself grinning.

"What is going on?" Cindy asked.

"Wait and see, but I can assure you, it's quite wonderful."

Fifteen minutes later Cindy turned away from the window where she had been staring at the babies. "You're right, it is quite wonderful."

"Well, now that you've met Rachel and Ryan, how about you say hi to Traci? They're finally letting her out of this place today. They kept her four days longer than either of us expected and we're going a bit crazy."

The reunion was a joyous one. Cindy and Traci kept hugging and crying and asking each other questions and then talking over each other. Mark found himself busy watching Jeremiah, though.

Jeremiah wasn't okay. Mark could tell just by glancing at him. It worried him a bit. "Rabbi, you all right?" he asked, purposely calling him by his title in an attempt to remind him of his current life instead of his old one.

Jeremiah didn't move, and Mark felt himself growing more anxious. "Rabbi!"

He shook his head and turned to Mark. He smiled, but it didn't reach his eyes which looked hard and cold.

Jeremiah moved closer to him. "What is it, Detective?"

Whereas he'd used Jeremiah's title to try to make him more at ease, Jeremiah used his to put distance between them.

"Dang it, man, don't do that to me," he said, keeping his voice low.

Jeremiah just stared at him.

"It really messed you up, didn't it?"

Jeremiah was silent and inwardly Mark cursed. All the progress they had made in trusting each other seemed to have been wiped out by a week-and-a-half of trouble.

Mark refused to back down. He locked his jaw and stared at the other man, willing Jeremiah to engage with him.

After nearly a minute Jeremiah blinked twice. His face relaxed, just for a moment. "Yes, it did," he whispered.

Then the cold, detached mask slipped back into place and Jeremiah turned back to the others.

Mark breathed a sigh of relief. The Jeremiah he knew wasn't dead, just really, really lost. Lost was something he understood. Once upon a time he'd been there himself. He could work with that.

He glanced at his watch. It was getting late back east.

"If all of you will excuse me a moment, there's a phone call I have to make."

Mark walked out into the hall and down to the room where the premature babies were. He stood outside and got out his phone. A moment later he was calling Asim's uncle in Detroit.

"Hello?"

"Mr. Kazmi, it's Detective Mark Walters."

"Detective, I was hoping to hear from you again."

"I promised I'd call when I had news," Mark said.

"You have found my nephew's killer?"

"I have found out who killed him, yes."

"And have you arrested him?"

"I couldn't. The people responsible for his death died a couple of days ago. In Israel."

There was a meaningful silence on the other end of the line. "Ah, I see," he said at last, very quietly and with sorrow in his voice.

"I am terribly sorry," Mark said.

"As am I. I told you, Detective, anger, hate they poison the mind and turn a man into a monster."

Mark could tell that the man understood that he had been telling him that Asim had been killed because of his brothers. "I am not at liberty to say very much."

"No one is these days it seems."

"I think there is something very important that you should know, though."

"I am listening."

"You know how you said you believed that Allah had spared him so that he might one day do something great?"

"Yes, he was a big believer in peace, and I always prayed he would help win the peace."

"He did."

"He did?" the man said, his voice full of wonder.

"Yes. He was killed because he was standing up for what was right. And his death actually gave us the information some people needed to stop a new world war from starting."

"Are you being truthful in this?" the man asked, hope starting to fill his voice.

"I am. His act of courage that led to his death, and your willingness to help me understand why he died were directly responsible for saving hundreds of thousands, if not millions of lives. You were right. Allah spared him when he was sixteen so that when he was twenty-one he could make the sacrifice that would save us all."

"We may not always know what action of ours today may affect others tomorrow."

"Or even the world," Mark added.

On the other end of the line Asim's uncle began crying and praying, part in English, part in Arabic, but Mark understood him perfectly clear. "Mr. Kazmi, you were right. He was a great man and there are many who will not forget what he has done."

"Thank you, thank you, you cannot know what this means to me. He was my nephew, but he lived in my house and I cared for him as if he were my own son. I loved him."

Mark turned his head so he could look at his two little angels, sleeping away. "I do understand," he said softly.

"If ever there is anything I can do for you, Detective, you will let me know."

"I will. Goodbye."

"Goodbye."

Mark hung up and struggled for a moment to get his own emotions under control. Calling Asim's uncle had been the least he could do. Now the man could be at peace and know that his nephew was the hero he'd always imagined he would be.

Now if he could just help Jeremiah find some peace everything would be right with the world.

Look for

TEX RAVENCROFT AND THE TEARS OF POSEIDON

By Debbie Viguié and Dr. Scott Viguié

Coming Summer 2014

Look for

I WILL FEAR NO EVIL

The next book in the Psalm 23 Mysteries series

Coming October 2014

Look for

THE SUMMER OF RICE CANDY

The next book in the Sweet Seasons series

Coming Fall 2014

Debbie Viguié is the New York Times Bestselling author of more thirty novels including the *Wicked* series, the *Crusade* series and the *Wolf Springs Chronicles* series co-authored with Nancy Holder. Debbie also writes thrillers including *The Psalm 23 Mysteries,* the *Kiss* trilogy, and the *Witch Hunt* trilogy. When Debbie isn't busy writing she enjoys spending time with her husband, Scott, visiting theme parks. They live in Florida with their cat, Schrödinger.

Made in the USA
San Bernardino, CA
12 June 2015